THE DEFINITIVE

STAR TREK®

TRIVIA BOOK

THE DEFINITIVE
STAR TREK®
TRIVIA BOOK

JILL SHERWIN

POCKET BOOKS

New York   London   Toronto   Sydney   Singapore   Memory Alpha

An *Original* Publication of POCKET BOOKS

 POCKET BOOKS, a division of Simon & Schuster Inc.
1230 Avenue of the Americas, New York, NY 10020

ISBN: 0-671-04182-7

First Pocket Books trade paperback printing April 2000

10 9 8 7 6 5 4 3 2 1

POCKET and colophon are registered trademarks of Simon & Schuster Inc.

Printed in the U.S.A.

To my mother, Judith Sherwin—
Together wherever we go

and

To Armin Shimerman,
my favorite Ferengi

CONTENTS

CONTENTS

SECTION ONE

STAR TREK®

THE ORIGINAL SERIES

JAMES T. KIRK

1. In "Where No Man Has Gone Before," what member of the *U.S.S. Enterprise* crew is mentioned to have attended Starfleet Academy with Kirk?
   (a) Gary Mitchell (b) Lee Kelso
   (c) Mark Piper (d) Elizabeth Dehner

2. Who was Kirk's nemesis at the academy?

3. What ship was Kirk's first assignment after graduating from the academy?

4. A transporter mishap created an evil duplicate of Kirk in which episode?
   (a) "Balance of Terror" (b) "The Devil in the Dark"
   (c) "The Enemy Within" (d) "Mirror, Mirror"

5. What did Kirk make from the raw materials on hand in "Arena"?

6. What creature's poison nearly killed Kirk in "A Private Little War"?

7. What name did an amnesiac Kirk go by in "The Paradise Syndrome"?

8. What disease did Kirk nearly die from as a child and later passed on in "The Mark of Gideon"?
   (a) Xenopolycythemia (b) Vegan choriomeningitis
   (c) Synthococcus novae (d) Rigellian Kassaba fever

9. In "The *Enterprise* Incident," what species did Kirk have himself surgically altered to look like?

10. Of whom did Abraham Lincoln say Kirk reminded him?

11. In "The Tholian Web," which two officers listened to Kirk's last taped orders?

12. As a young man, Kirk survived the massacre of 4,000 colonists on what planet?

SPOCK

13. True or false: Spock served aboard the *Enterprise* longer than Kirk, Leonard McCoy, or Montgomery Scott.

14. What was Spock's dual position aboard the *Enterprise?*

15. The Horta found what aspect of Spock's appearance most appealing?

16. In "Return to Tomorrow," where was Spock's consciousness hidden when Henoch destroyed the globe-shaped vessel that contained it?

17. What is Spock's blood type?

18. What was Spock's mother's profession?

19. Name Spock's fiancée.

20. Whom did she wish to marry instead?

21. Who opposed Spock's choice to serve in Starfleet?
(a) T'Pau (b) T'Pring (c) Amanda (d) Sarek

22. Spock was blinded in what episode?
(a) "Is There in Truth No Beauty?"
(b) "Operation: Annihilate!"
(c) "A Taste of Armageddon"
(d) "The Alternative Factor"

23. What level computer expert classification does Spock hold?
(a) A7 (b) B9 (c) A12 (d) Delta Vega

24. In which episode did Spock first wear an IDIC symbol?
(a) "Journey to Babel"
(b) "Amok Time"
(c) "The Savage Curtain"
(d) "Is There in Truth No Beauty?"

LEONARD MCCOY

25. What was Kirk's nickname for McCoy?

26. What was Nancy Crater's nickname for McCoy?

27. What was McCoy's position aboard the *Enterprise?*

28. In which episode did McCoy require Kirk to eat a salad?
(a) "The Corbomite Maneuver"   (b) "Arena"
(c) "Balance of Terror"   (d) "Charlie X"

29. In which episode did McCoy "finally get the last word"?
(a) "A Private Little War"   (b) "This Side of Paradise"
(c) "Journey to Babel"   (d) "The *Enterprise* Incident"

30. What two characters from a children's novel did McCoy see in "Shore Leave"?

31. By whom was McCoy apparently killed in "Shore Leave"?

32. Name the gladiator McCoy fought in "Bread and Circuses."
(a) Septimus   (b) Flavius
(c) Claudius   (d) Merikus

33. With what medication did McCoy accidentally inject himself in "The City on the Edge of Forever"?

34. McCoy delivered a baby on what planet?
(a) Capella IV   (b) Omega IV   (c) Omicron Ceti III
(d) Sarpeidon

35. What particular piece of *Enterprise* equipment was McCoy especially disdainful of using?
(a) Shuttlecraft   (b) Phaser   (c) Transporter
(d) Computer

36. Name the woman McCoy married during *The Original Series.*

MONTGOMERY SCOTT

37. What was Scott's position aboard the *Enterprise?*

38. Scott was always concerned about the condition of his
(a) **Captain** (b) **Shipmates** (c) **Engines**
(d) **Employment**

39. In what episode was Scott struck by what looks like a lightning bolt?
(a) **"Charlie X"** (b) **"Wolf in the Fold"**
(c) **"The Apple"** (d) **"Who Mourns for Adonais?"**

40. In what A&A officer was Scott romantically interested?
(a) **Lieutenant Mira Romaine**
(b) **Lieutenant Carolyn Palamas**
(c) **Lieutenant Marla McGivers**
(d) **Lieutenant Uhura**

41. Which two officers took Scotty down to Argelius II for shore leave?

42. What killed Scott and then returned him to life?

43. What are Scott's favorite reading materials?

44. What do the Klingons insult to provoke Scott in "The Trouble With Tribbles"?

45. What is Scott's weapon of choice against Tomar in "By Any Other Name"?

46. In "Whom Gods Destroy," what security code did Scott use, per Kirk's orders?
(a) **King to King's Level Three**
(b) **Queen to Queen's Level Three**
(c) **King to Queen's Level Three**
(d) **Queen to King's Level Three**

47. In which of these episodes was Scott heard but *not* seen?
   (a) "City on the Edge of Forever"
   (b) "All Our Yesterdays"
   (c) "Court Martial"
   (d) "The Cage"

48. Scott was
   (a) Icelandic (b) British (c) Irish (d) Scottish

HIKARU SULU

49. Name the episode in which Sulu first appeared.

50. In that same episode, Sulu's job was
(a) **Helmsman** (b) **Physicist** (c) **Transporter chief**
(d) **Security officer**

51. In which episode did Sulu almost die of exposure to subzero cold?
(a) **"The Enemy Within"** (b) **"The Naked Time"**
(c) **"All Our Yesterdays"** (d) **"Space Seed"**

52. Name Sulu's plant in "The Man Trap."

53. In "The Naked Time," Sulu ran around the ship with what weapon?

54. By what machine was Sulu "absorbed"?
(a) **M-5** (b) **Norman** (c) *Nomad* (d) **Landru**

55. In "Shore Leave," Sulu is chased by
(a) **Strafing airplanes** (b) **A large white rabbit**
(c) **A samurai** (d) **A knight on horseback**

56. Which episode opens with Sulu running for his life?

57. What physical feature distinguishes the mirror universe Sulu from the Sulu of our own universe?

58. In "Tomorrow Is Yesterday," Sulu joins Kirk on a mission to steal what?

59. In which one of the following episodes is Sulu seen commanding the *Enterprise?*
(a) **"Balance of Terror"**
(b) **"Errand of Mercy"**
(c) **"The Squire of Gothos"**
(d) **"A Taste of Armageddon"**

60. Sulu was saved by a few drops of cordrazine in what episode?

UHURA

61. Besides English, what other language was Uhura known to speak?

62. Which was the only episode in which Uhura wore a gold uniform?
  (a) "Mudd's Women"
  (b) "Court Martial"
  (c) "The Corbomite Maneuver"
  (d) "The Man Trap"

63. Which crew member does Uhura tease with a song in "Charlie X"?

64. What did *Nomad* do to Uhura?

65. With whom does Uhura flirt in "Mirror, Mirror"?

66. With what do the androids tempt Uhura in "I, Mudd"?

67. While on leave on Deep Space Station K-7, Uhura wanted to go
  (a) Swimming (b) Dancing (c) Shopping
  (d) Rock climbing

68. Who went along with Uhura to K-7?

69. Who was Uhura's drill thrall in "The Gamesters of Triskelion"?
  (a) Shahna (b) Galt (c) Lars (d) Tamoon

70. To whom did Uhura lend her cabin in "Elaan of Troyius"?
  (a) Elaan (b) Petri (c) Kryton
  (d) The ruler of Troyius

71. What fear of Uhura's is shown in "And the Children Shall Lead"?

72. Who did Uhura kiss in "Plato's Stepchildren"?

PAVEL CHEKOV

73. What was Chekov's job aboard the *Enterprise?*

74. Chekov firmly believed that everything was a _____ invention.

75. According to Chekov, Scotch whiskey was invented by a little old lady from _____.

76. What frightened Chekov in "The Deadly Years"?

77. With whom did Chekov flirt in "The Apple"?
(a) Yeoman Tamura (b) Yeoman Rand
(c) Yeoman Mears (d) Yeoman Landon

78. In "The Trouble With Tribbles," who was assigned to keep Chekov out of trouble on Deep Space Station K-7?

79. On the bridge, whose station did Chekov often man when it was vacated?
(a) Kirk's (b) Spock's (c) Scott's (d) Uhura's

80. Who was Chekov's drill thrall in "The Gamesters of Triskelion"?
(a) Shahna (b) Galt (c) Lars (d) Tamoon

81. Name the episode in which Chekov was apparently killed.

82. Who was his love interest in the same episode?

83. What was the name of Chekov's phantom brother in "Day of the Dove"?
(a) Yuri (b) Misha (c) Piotr (d) Boris

84. Name the Starfleet cadet with whom Chekov was romantically involved before she dropped out of the academy.

RECURRING AND GUEST CHARACTERS

85. With which crew member was Christine Chapel infatuated?

86. Name Chapel's long-lost fiancé.

87. What was Chapel's job?

88. Chapel was blond in every episode she appeared in except one, in which her hair was brown. That episode was
   (a) "The Lights of Zetar"
   (b) "Turnabout Intruder"
   (c) "Spock's Brain"
   (d) "The Gamesters of Triskelion"

89. Name the two episodes in which Kevin Riley appeared.

90. Riley was very proud of his _____ heritage.

91. While infected by the Psi 2000 virus, Riley locked himself in _____ and declared himself captain of the *Enterprise*.

92. Where were Riley's parents killed?
   (a) Tarsus IV   (b) Deneb V
   (c) Gamma Hydra IV   (d) Earth Colony 2

93. Dr. M'Benga was a
   (a) Psychiatrist   (b) Physician   (c) Dentist
   (d) Anesthesiologist

94. Where did Dr. M'Benga intern?
   (a) Vulcan   (b) Altair   (c) Deneva   (d) Mars

95. Name the two episodes in which Dr. M'Benga appeared.

96. Who was under Dr. M'Benga's care after receiving a gunshot wound?

97. What was Harry Mudd's full name?

98. In which two episodes did Mudd appear?

99. The first time Mudd appeared, what alias did he use?

100. What was Mudd's wife's name?
(a) Alice (b) Trudy (c) Stella (d) T'Pring

101. In "The Cage," which of the following does Captain Pike *not* come up with as a possibility for a career change?
(a) Go home (b) Go into business on Regulus
(c) Sell tribbles (d) Become an Orion trader

102. Who was left in command of the *Enterprise* while Captain Pike led the landing party?

103. Who was the only survivor of the *S.S. Columbia* when it crashed on Talos IV?

104. In "Where No Man Has Gone Before," the *Enterprise*'s chief medical officer was
(a) Dr. Van Gelder (b) Dr. Boyce (c) Dr. Dehner
(d) Dr. Piper

105. In "The Corbomite Maneuver," who was the crewman who stayed on Balok's ship for the purpose of cultural exchange?

106. Name the civilization to which Balok's ship belonged.

107. Into what animal did Charlie transform Yeoman Tina Lawton?
(a) Iguana (b) Cat (c) Tribble (d) Monkey

108. Name the episode in which a shipboard wedding ceremony was interrupted.

109. Who was prejudiced against Spock in "Balance of Terror"?
(a) Stiles (b) DeSalle (c) Tomlinson
(d) Tormolen

110. What destroyed the Old Ones of Exo III?

111. What was the name of the female android built by Dr. Roger Korby?
(a) Alice (b) Andrea (c) Rayna (d) Lethe

112. Name the android that transferred Dr. Korby's mind into an android body.

113. Who killed Anton Karidian?

114. Whom did Kirk suspect Anton Karidian to be?

115. What was the name of Ben Finney's daughter?

116. For whom was she named?

117. Kirk served under the command of the father of which *Enterprise* crew member?

118. Name the twentieth-century U.S. Air Force pilot who spotted the *Enterprise* in Earth's atmosphere.

119. How many "witches" tried to warn off the landing party in "Catspaw"?

120. In "Space Seed," who was the *Enterprise* historian who chose to join Khan?
(a) Lieutenant Carolyn Palamas (b) John Gill
(c) Dr. Helen Noel (d) Lieutenant Marla McGivers

121. Khan was the absolute ruler of how much of Earth?
(a) Three quarters (b) One half (c) One third
(d) One quarter

122. In "Wolf in the Fold," Mr. Hengist came from what planet?
(a) Alpha Carinae V (b) Alpha Majoris I
(c) Argelius II (d) Rigel IV

123. By what name was the Redjac entity known on Earth?

124. By whom is Yeoman Tonia Barrows attacked in "Shore Leave"?

STAR TREK: THE ORIGINAL SERIES

125. Whom did Kirk fight in "Arena"?

126. Who set up the battle in "Arena"?

127. Which of these items did Cyrano Jones *not* try to sell
to the bartender on Deep Space Station K-7?
(a) **Spican flame gems**   (b) **Kevas and trillium**
(c) **Antarian Glow Water**   (d) **Tribbles**

128. In "Metamorphosis," with whom did the Companion
merge?

129. In "Who Mourns for Adonais?" which Greek god
captured the *Enterprise?*
(a) **Zeus**   (b) **Artemis**   (c) **Ares**   (d) **Apollo**

130. In "The Apple," who was the leader of the people
who fed Vaal?

131. In "Assignment: Earth," who were the two agents
whose progress Gary Seven was sent to check?
(a) **806 and 912**   (b) **201 and 347**   (c) **14 and 007**
(d) **86 and 99**

132. For whom is "Gary Seven" a code name?

133. In "Plato's Stepchildren," which Platonian did *not*
have telekinetic powers?

134. In "Requiem for Methuselah," what was the name of
Flint's android?

135. In "All Our Yesterdays," who operated the atavachron?

136. Who condemned Zarabeth to exile?

137. Which of the following women was *not* attracted to
Spock?
(a) **The Romulan commander**   (b) **Leila Kalomi**
(c) **Helen Noel**   (d) **Droxine**

138. Who commanded Starbase 11 in "Court Martial"?
(a) **Commodore Stone**   (b) **Commodore Mendez**
(c) **Commodore Stocker**   (d) **Commodore Wesley**

139. Who was described as a "work of art" in "The Cloud Minders"?

140. In "Is There in Truth No Beauty?" Dr. Miranda Jones was
(a) Deaf   (b) Mute   (c) Blind   (d) Paralyzed

THE ORIGINAL *ENTERPRISE*

141. How many people were aboard the *Enterprise* when Pike was captain?
(a) 203   (b) 428   (c) 430   (d) 1,012

142. Which class of starship was the original *Enterprise?*
(a) *Constellation*   (b) *Constitution*   (c) *Excelsior*
(d) *Galaxy*

143. When the *Enterprise* travels faster than the speed of light, this is called _____ speed.

144. Warp propulsion was made possible in part by _____ crystals.

145. In "Mudd's Women," these crystals were referred to by a slightly different name. What was it?

146. Scotty was often climbing into access tunnels known as _____ .

147. What was the weapons storage area aboard the *Enterprise* called?

148. From what room could the ship be run in an emergency?

149. With what *Enterprise* facility did Khan threaten Kirk's life?

150. In "The Apple," what emergency procedure does Kirk order for freeing the *Enterprise* if all else fails?
(a) Warp engine implosion   (b) Slingshot maneuver
(c) Saucer separation   (d) Impulse engine overload

151. In "Is There in Truth No Beauty," one of the original designers of the *Enterprise* comes aboard. The engineer's name is
(a) Commander Orfil Quinteros
(b) Dr. Laurence Marvick
(c) Dr. Leah Brahms
(d) Dr. Miranda Jones

152. Which of the following was mentioned to exist
aboard the *Enterprise?*
(a) Racquetball court   (b) Dance hall
(c) Bowling alley   (d) Firing range

CRAZED CAPTAINS

153. In "The Doomsday Machine," who was the commanding officer of the *U.S.S. Constellation?*

154. What was his rank?

155. What ship captain became first citizen of a parallel Roman Empire in "Bread and Circuses"?

156. In "Whom Gods Destroy," the shape-changing technique used by Garth of Izar was called
(a) **Cellular metamorphosis** (b) **Shape-shifting**
(c) **Metagenesis** (d) **Molecular realignment**

157. Garth proclaimed himself
(a) **Lord Garth** (b) **King Garth**
(c) **Emperor Garth** (d) **The Divine Garth**

158. Garth's followers did *not* include
(a) **An Andorian** (b) **A Vulcan** (c) **A Tellarite**
(d) **An Orion**

159. In "The Omega Glory," Ronald Tracey was captain of what starship?
(a) *U.S.S. Endeavour* (b) *U.S.S. Excelsior*
(c) *U.S.S. Exeter* (d) *U.S.S. Excalibur*

160. Tracey violated what Federation law?

161. Tracey believed that planet Omega IV held the key to

———.

162. In "Turnabout Intruder," who fulfilled her dreams of starship command by forcibly switching bodies with Kirk?

163. In "The Enemy Within," the "evil" Kirk demanded what from McCoy?

164. In "The *Enterprise* Incident," a seemingly insane Kirk was apparently killed by Spock with what bogus technique?

SUPERCOMPUTERS

165. In "The Return of the Archons," which of the following characters was *not* absorbed by Landru?
(a) Kirk   (b) McCoy   (c) Sulu
(d) Lieutenant O'Neil

166. If you were absorbed by Landru, you were
(a) Of the Mind   (b) Of the Body
(c) Of the Collective   (d) Landru's children

167. Name the two planets that fought a war via computers in "A Taste of Armageddon."

168. In "The Changeling," who was revealed to be *Nomad*'s creator?

169. What alien robot probe did *Nomad* encounter after being damaged?
(a) Ba'ku   (b) Mab-Bu   (c) Gomtuu   (d) *Tan Ru*

170. In "The Apple," what computer relied on the primitive people of Gamma Trianguli VI to provide it with sustenance?

171. What computer system used a humanoid brain to sustain the subterranean environment of the Eymorg?

172. Whose brain was stolen to run this system?

173. What was the name of the multitronic computer that took control of the *Enterprise?*
(a) B-9   (b) K-7   (c) M-4   (d) M-5

174. In "The Ultimate Computer," who created a computer system intended to replace starship captains?

175. In "For the World Is Hollow and I Have Touched the Sky," name the computer who enforced the laws of *Yonada.*

176. In "Tomorrow Is Yesterday," it was revealed that the *Enterprise* computer had been provided with a female personality by the technicians of what planet?
(a) Ingraham B   (b) Cygnet XIV
(c) Berengaria VII   (d) Talos IV

THE CAPTAIN'S WOMEN

177. In "Dagger of the Mind," Dr. Adams placed the suggestion in Kirk's mind that he was in love with which crewmate?
(a) Janice Rand   (b) Marla McGivers
(c) Helen Noel   (d) Marlena Moreau

178. What centuries-old adolescent developed a crush on Kirk when he visited her planet?

179. In "The Deadly Years," an aging Kirk is helped by his former girlfriend. She was
(a) Janet Wallace   (b) Ruth   (c) Areel Shaw
(d) Dr. Carol Marcus

180. What was Areel Shaw's profession?

181. In "Mirror, Mirror," who was the "captain's woman" of the alternate Kirk?

182. In "Shore Leave," which of Kirk's ex-girlfriends does Kirk seem to encounter?

183. Who was starring in the movie Edith Keeler wanted to see with Kirk in "The City on the Edge of Forever"?
(a) Errol Flynn   (b) Spencer Tracy
(c) Clark Gable   (d) Humphrey Bogart

184. In "By Any Other Name," Kelinda's people came from what galaxy?

185. What was Elaan's title as leader of Elas?
(a) Empress   (b) Duchess   (c) Dauphin
(d) Dohlman

186. In "The Mark of Gideon," with whom was Kirk trapped on a phony *Enterprise?*
(a) Odona   (b) Deela   (c) Vanna   (d) Kara

187. Who thought Kirk would be an ideal mate in "Wink of an Eye"?

(a) **Odona**　(b) **Deela**　(c) **Vanna**　(d) **Kara**

188. In one episode of *The Original Series,* Kirk got married. Name his wife.

MISCELLANEOUS DATA

189. Who was the only character to cross over from the original pilot, "The Cage," to the regular series?

190. What was the duration of the *Enterprise*'s original mission under Kirk?

191. Which of the following did *not* happen because of the disease contracted on Psi 2000?
(a) **Spock cried.**   (b) **Sulu fenced.**
(c) **Riley sang.**   (d) **Uhura danced.**

192. In "The Man Trap," the M-113 creature needed _____ to survive.

193. How many colonists did Kodos the Executioner condemn to death?

194. What creature did Spock imagine he saw in the clouds of Omicron Ceti III?

195. Match the following *Enterprise* crew members with the alien consciousnesses who possessed them in "Return to Tomorrow":
(a) **Kirk**   i. **Henoch**
(b) **Spock**   ii. **Thalassa**
(c) **Dr. Ann Mulhall**   iii. **Sargon**

196. Which *Enterprise* crew member had been to Capella IV prior to events in "Friday's Child"?
(a) **Kirk**   (b) **Spock**   (c) **McCoy**   (d) **Scott**

197. In "Plato's Stepchildren," the Platonians' gift to Kirk was a _____.

198. With what game did Kirk distract his captors in "A Piece of the Action"?

199. In "The Cloud Minders," by what name were the miners of Ardana known?

200. What color shirt did you *not* want to be wearing if you were part of a landing party?

SECTION TWO

JEAN-LUC PICARD

1. The first ship Picard commanded was the _____.

2. Picard has an artificial
(a) **Eye** (b) **Lung** (c) **Heart** (d) **Leg**

3. Whom did Picard once call "next of kin to chaos"?

4. When Picard was assimilated by the Borg, his designation was _____.

5. What job did Admiral Quinn offer to Picard in "Coming of Age"?
(a) **Commander of Utopia Planitia Fleet Yards**
(b) **Commandant of Starfleet Academy**
(c) **Chief of Starfleet Intelligence**
(d) **Ambassador to Romulus**

6. What initials did Picard carve into Boothby's prize elm tree?

7. Picard's family owned
(a) **A horse ranch** (b) **Vineyards** (c) **A castle**
(d) **An island**

8. In "Family," what civilian endeavor was Picard invited to supervise on Earth?

9. Name Picard's former archaeology professor.

10. What gift does Picard receive from the Mintakans in "Who Watches the Watchers?"

11. For what personal item did Picard return to the *Enterprise*-D in "Starship Mine"?
(a) **A saddle** (b) **A foil** (c) **A book** (d) **A flute**

12. Picard's beverage of choice was
(a) **Coffee** (b) *Raktajino* (c) **Earl Grey tea**
(d) **Synthehol**

STAR TREK: THE NEXT GENERATION

WILLIAM T. RIKER

13. Who was Riker's captain just prior to Picard?

14. On what planet did Riker and Deanna Troi first meet and fall in love?
(a) **Risa**   (b) **Betazed**   (c) **Pacifica**   (d) **Angel One**

15. By what title did Picard frequently address Riker?
(a) **First Officer**   (b) **Exec**   (c) **X.O.**
(d) **Number One**

16. Whom did Riker address as "Pinocchio" in "Encounter at Farpoint, Part I"?

17. In "11001001," with what holodeck character did Riker become fascinated?

18. In preparation for his assignment to serve aboard a Klingon ship, Riker
(a) **Dressed like a Klingon**
(b) **Practiced with a *bat'leth***
(c) **Ate Klingon food**
(d) **Practiced speaking Klingon**

19. Which of the following ships did Riker *not* serve aboard?
(a) *U.S.S. Ajax*   (b) *U.S.S. Hood*
(c) *U.S.S. Pegasus*   (d) *U.S.S. Potemkin*

20. Which of the following ships was Riker *not* offered command of?
(a) *U.S.S. Aries*   (b) *U.S.S. Drake*   (c) *U.S.S. Gandhi*
(d) *U.S.S. Melbourne*

21. In what style of futuristic martial arts did Riker and his father share skill?
(a) *Mok'bara*   (b) Anbo-jytsu   (c) *Tal-shaya*
(d) **Galeo-Manada**

25

22. Into what kind of life-form did Riker regress in "Evolution"?
(a) Primitive human   (b) Reptile   (c) Arachnid
(d) Amphibian

23. Who was after Riker's job in "The Best of Both Worlds"?

24. William T. Riker's middle initial stands for
(a) Thaddeus   (b) Thelonius   (c) Thomas
(d) Tiberius

DATA

25. Name the colony where Data was created.

26. Which two people built Data?

27. What was Data's rank?

28. In "Hide and Q," the Q-empowered Riker offered to fulfill Data's fondest wish. What was it?

29. In which episode was it learned that Data had an off switch?

30. Who was Data's closest friend?

31. Who was Data's girlfriend during "In Theory"?
  (a) **Lieutenant Aquiel Uhnari**
  (b) **Lieutenant Jenna D'Sora**
  (c) **Sito Jaxa**
  (d) **Alyssa Ogawa**

32. In which episode did Data first command a starship?

33. What ship did he command?

34. In what episode was Data's disembodied head found buried in San Francisco?

35. Data's brain is
  (a) **Duotronic**   (b) **Multitronic**   (c) **Positronic**
  (d) **Hypertronic**

36. True or false: Data's hair grows.

WORF

37. On what world were Worf's biological parents killed?

38. Worf's biological father was named
(a) **Martok** (b) **Mogh** (c) **Ja'rod** (d) **K'mpec**

39. Who was Worf's nursemaid when he was a child?

40. Who was known to address Worf as "Mr. Woof"?

41. On what planet was Worf raised by his foster parents?
(a) **Gault** (b) **Earth** (c) **Mars** (d) **Veridian III**

42. Name the mother of Worf's son.

43. Name Worf's son.

44. Who first suggested that Worf try prune juice?
(a) **Deanna Troi** (b) **Guinan** (c) **Riker**
(d) **Picard**

45. In "QPid," what does Worf insist that he is *not?*

46. What part of Worf's body was injured in "Ethics"?
(a) **His arm** (b) **His chest** (c) **His spine**
(d) **His leg**

47. What kind of competition did Worf win in "Parallels"?

48. Which character in "Lower Decks" was Worf's protégée?
(a) **Sito Jaxa** (b) **Ro Laren** (c) **Jenna D'Sora**
(d) **Ensign Robin Lefler**

DEANNA TROI

49. What was Troi's job?

50. Troi's father was
(a) A Betazoid ambassador   (b) A winemaker
(c) A psychologist   (d) A Starfleet officer

51. What was Lwaxana's nickname for Deanna?

52. In "Haven," who was Troi's fiancé?

53. What did Troi name her son in "The Child"?
(a) Ian Aaron   (b) Ivan Andrew
(c) Ian Andrew   (d) Ivan Aaron

54. Troi was primarily
(a) Telepathic   (b) Telekinetic   (c) Pyrokinetic
(d) Empathic

55. With whom did Troi become romantically involved in
"The Price"?
(a) Devinoni Ral   (b) DaiMon Bok
(c) Tam Elbrun   (d) Worf

56. In what episode does Troi fall for a genetically engineered human?
(a) "The Price"
(b) "Evolution"
(c) "Man of the People"
(d) "The Masterpiece Society"

57. In what episode is Troi trapped on the bridge and in command of the ship?

58. In "Face of the Enemy," Troi was kidnapped and surgically altered to look like a member of what species?

59. What book of poetry did Troi once give Riker that she inscribed "To Will, all my love, Deanna"?

60. In "Thine Own Self," to what rank is Troi promoted?

GEORDI LA FORGE

61. What device enables a blind La Forge to "see"?

62. On what starship did La Forge serve under Captain Zimbata?
(a) *U.S.S. Victory* (b) *U.S.S. Valiant*
(c) *U.S.S. Defiant* (d) *U.S.S. Reliant*

63. La Forge started out on the *Enterprise*-D as what?
(a) **Flight controller** (b) **Operations manager**
(c) **Chief engineer** (d) **Tactical officer**

64. To what position was La Forge later promoted?
(a) **Flight controller** (b) **Operations manager**
(c) **Chief engineer** (d) **Tactical officer**

65. In what episode did La Forge command the *Enterprise*-D's "battle section"?

66. Whom did Guinan suggest that La Forge befriend in "Hollow Pursuits"?

67. In "Disaster," for what play did Dr. Beverly Crusher want La Forge to audition?
(a) *Frame of Mind* (b) *Cyrano de Bergerac*
(c) *Henry V* (d) *The Pirates of Penzance*

68. La Forge once became attracted to a woman through a holorecreation. Name her.

69. In "QPid," La Forge assumed the role of which member of Robin Hood's followers?
(a) **Will Scarlet** (b) **Alan-a-Dale** (c) **Friar Tuck**
(d) **Little John**

70. What language did La Forge learn to better understand Aquiel Uhnari?
(a) **Haliian** (b) **Bajoran** (c) **Sheliak** (d) **French**

71. What Starfleet rank was La Forge's mother?

72. In "The Mind's Eye," La Forge is brainwashed by members of what species?

BEVERLY CRUSHER

73. Who introduced Jack Crusher to Beverly?
(a) Jean-Luc Picard   (b) Walker Keel
(c) Dr. Dalen Quaice   (d) Sarek

74. On what planet was Crusher when she joined the crew of the *Enterprise*-D?

75. For what assignment did Crusher leave the *Enterprise*-D for a year?

76. What skill did Crusher teach Data in preparation for the O'Briens' wedding?

77. Crusher regularly enjoyed what meal with Picard?
(a) Breakfast   (b) Lunch   (c) Dinner
(d) Midnight snack

78. In the episode "Remember Me," Crusher found herself trapped in a universe that was
(a) Rapidly expanding   (b) Rapidly contracting
(c) Rapidly aging   (d) Frozen in time

79. What was Crusher's maiden name?

80. What heirloom was handed down in Crusher's family from mother to daughter?
(a) Candle   (b) Book   (c) Mirror   (d) Chalice

81. Crusher's grandmother was
(a) An engineer   (b) A healer   (c) A psychic
(d) A homemaker

82. On what planet did a young Beverly Crusher and her grandmother survive a colonywide disaster?
(a) Turkana IV   (b) Tarsus IV   (c) Arvada III
(d) Angel One

83. In "Attached," Crusher learned that Picard had once been
   (a) In love with her
   (b) Responsible for Jack Crusher's death
   (c) Against her assignment to the *Enterprise*-D
   (d) Uncomfortable around children

84. In what episode did Crusher command the *Enterprise*-D?
   (a) "The Best of Both Worlds, Part II"
   (b) "Unification, Part II"
   (c) "Descent, Part II"
   (d) "All Good Things . . ."

WESLEY CRUSHER

85. In the episode "Justice," Wesley was sentenced to death for

(a) Stepping on flowers

(b) Stealing

(c) Talking to children

(d) Insulting a member of another species

86. True or false: One of Wesley's class projects once resulted in the creation of a self-aware hologram.

87. In "The Dauphin," which two people demonstrated the art of flirting to Wesley?

(a) Riker and Troi   (b) Geordi and Ro

(c) Riker and Guinan   (d) Geordi and Troi

88. Who consoled Wesley by admitting that he, too, once failed the Starfleet Academy entrance exam?

89. In which episode was Wesley made acting ensign?

90. In which episode was Wesley made a full ensign?

91. Wesley's usual post was

(a) Ops   (b) Tactical   (c) Sciences II   (d) Conn

92. In what episode did Wesley attempt to conceal the truth behind the death of a Starfleet cadet?

93. In "Journey's End," Wesley departed with

(a) The Maquis   (b) Q   (c) The Traveler

(d) The Prophets

94. In "Final Mission," whose life did Wesley save?

95. The elite flight team to which Wesley belonged at Starfleet Academy was

(a) Red Squad   (b) Nova Squadron   (c) Section 31

(d) Alpha Squad

96. In one of the alternate quantum realities of "Parallels," Wesley Crusher was seen on the *Enterprise*-D bridge at what post?

NATASHA YAR

97. What was Yar's job on the *Enterprise*-D?

98. To whom did Yar make amorous advances in "The Naked Now"?

99. What was the name of Yar's home planet?

100. Yar's nickname was _____.

101. True or false: Yar was raised by Romulans.

102. Who killed Yar?
(a) **Q** (b) **Armus** (c) **Romulans** (d) **Klingons**

103. The daughter of an alternate Yar was born and raised in this universe. What was her name?

104. This daughter's father was a
(a) **Romulan** (b) **Klingon** (c) **Cardassian**
(d) **Breen**

105. Who replaced Yar as chief of security?

106. True or false: Yar's home planet was a failed Federation colony.

107. In which of the following episodes did Yar *not* appear?
(a) **"Code of Honor"** (b) **"A Matter of Honor"**
(c) **"Heart of Glory"** (d) **"The Last Outpost"**

108. Yar was killed on
(a) **Ventax II** (b) **Volon II** (c) **Vagra II**
(d) **Vilmor II**

RECURRING AND GUEST CHARACTERS

109. Whom did Katherine Pulaski replace when she was assigned to the *Enterprise*-D?

110. With which *Enterprise*-D crew member's father did Pulaski have a prior relationship?

111. How many times was Pulaski married?

112. On what starship did Pulaski serve prior to the *Enterprise*-D?
(a) *U.S.S. Reliant* (b) *U.S.S. Republic*
(c) *U.S.S. Repulse* (d) *U.S.S. Revere*

113. Pulaski once joined Data in what holodeck scenario?

114. Pulaski was disdainful of what particular form of transportation?

115. Reginald Barclay's job was
(a) **Engineer** (b) **Physicist** (c) **Biologist**
(d) **Doctor**

116. From what condition did Barclay *not* suffer?
(a) **Shyness** (b) **Holo-addiction**
(c) **Transporter psychosis** (d) **Bendii syndrome**

117. What holoprogram did Barclay help Alexander develop?

118. In "The Nth Degree," which of the following aspects of Barclay was *not* enhanced?
(a) **His intellect** (b) **His strength**
(c) **His confidence** (d) **His romantic/social skills**

119. Which of the following species used Barclay to make contact with the Federation?
(a) **Cytherians** (b) **D'Arsay** (c) **J'naii** (d) **Tkon**

120. What disease was named for Barclay?
   (a) Barclay's arachnoid metamorphosis
   (b) Barclay's holographic disorder
   (c) Barclay's protomorphosis syndrome
   (d) Barclay's transporter psychosis

121. Miles O'Brien first appeared in what episode?

122. Whom did O'Brien marry?

123. Who delivered O'Brien's daughter?

124. O'Brien's attitude toward Cardassians was profoundly affected by a massacre on what planet?
   (a) Khitomer   (b) Narendra III   (c) Bajor
   (d) Setlik III

125. O'Brien served previously under Captain Maxwell of what starship?
   (a) *U.S.S. Yorktown*   (b) *U.S.S. Stargazer*
   (c) *U.S.S. Rutledge*   (d) *U.S.S. Phoenix*

126. On that ship, O'Brien's job was
   (a) Chief engineer   (b) Tactical officer
   (c) Transporter chief   (d) Operations manager

127. Where did Guinan tend bar aboard the *Enterprise*-D?

128. Guinan is known to have visited Earth in what century?
   (a) Twentieth   (b) Nineteenth   (c) Eighteenth
   (d) Seventeenth

129. By whom was Guinan's homeworld destroyed?

130. True or false: Guinan had children.

131. According to Guinan, who was the only other member of her family to have a sense of humor?
   (a) Terkim   (b) Martus   (c) Soran   (d) Tain

132. Guinan's people were known best as
   (a) Advisers   (b) Listeners   (c) Wanderers
   (d) Explorers

133. What woman did Picard meet while vacationing on Risa?

134. With whom did she elect to travel the universe?

135. Who was Dr. Crusher's nurse aboard the *Enterprise*-D?
(a) Sito Jaxa (b) Simon Tarses (c) Alyssa Ogawa
(d) Taurik

136. Although he is not mentioned by name, which member of the original *Enterprise* crew toured the *Enterprise*-D in "Encounter at Farpoint, Part I"?

137. What creature attacked the Omicron Theta colony?

138. Who led the Klingon Empire longer than anyone in history?
(a) Kahless (b) Gorkon (c) Mogh (d) K'mpec

139. Who was possessed by the "mother" parasite in "Conspiracy"?
(a) Tryla Scott (b) Gregory Quinn
(c) Dexter Remmick (d) Walker Keel

140. Name the *Enterprise*-D's Vulcan doctor.

141. Name the *Enterprise*-D's barber.

142. Name the first Bajoran to serve aboard the *Enterprise*-D.

143. On the *Enterprise*-D, Keiko was a
(a) Starfleet nurse (b) Starfleet biologist
(c) Civilian botanist (d) Civilian schoolteacher

144. What Romulan commander spearheaded efforts to destabilize the Klingon–Federation alliance as well as a scheme to invade Vulcan?

THE *U.S.S. ENTERPRISE* NCC-1701-D

145. The *Enterprise*-D was what class of starship?

146. Name the shipyards where the *Enterprise*-D was built.

147. The name of the officer in charge of the *Enterprise*-D assembly team was
(a) **Leah Brahms**   (b) **Orfil Quinteros**
(c) **Erik Pressman**   (d) **Alynna Nechayev**

148. The *Enterprise*-D had a crew of over _____.

149. What was the small captain's office just off the bridge called?

150. Where was the ship's main shuttlebay located?
(a) **On the front of the saucer**
(b) **On the back of the saucer**
(c) **On the front of the drive section**
(d) **On the back of the drive section**

151. When a saucer separation is ordered, the drive section is commanded from the _____.

152. In the episode "Reunion," Picard said that the *Enterprise*-D crew included representatives of how many planets?
(a) **13**   (b) **24**   (c) **27**   (d) **62**

153. Picard was once reassigned. Name the Starfleet captain who replaced him as commanding officer of the *Enterprise*-D.

154. Who was second officer of the *Enterprise*-D?

155. Name the episode in which the *Enterprise*-D uses a cloaking device.

156. In which episode was the *Enterprise*-D destroyed repeatedly?

Q

157. In "Encounter at Farpoint," Q wears a judge's attire from what century?

(a) Seventeenth   (b) Eighteenth   (c) Twentieth
(d) Twenty-first

158. True or false: Q once appeared to Picard in a stream of cigar smoke.

159. With what did Q once tempt Riker?

(a) Wealth   (b) Starship command
(c) The power of the Q   (d) His true love

160. In "Q Who?" Q returns to the *Enterprise*-D because

(a) He wants to destroy it
(b) He wants to join the crew
(c) He needs Picard's help
(d) He has to avert a disaster

161. In the same episode, with whom was it revealed that Q had had a previous encounter?

162. What species did Q once call "the ultimate user"?

163. When Q was made mortal as punishment for his behavior, what species sought revenge against him?

(a) Romulans   (b) Sheliak   (c) Husnock
(d) Calamarain

164. In "QPid," what role in the reenactment of *The Adventures of Robin Hood* does Q play?

165. In "True Q," whom does Q say is becoming "more shrill with each passing year"?

(a) Riker   (b) Crusher   (c) Troi   (d) Worf

166. In the same episode, Q wanted to take Amanda Rogers to the Q Continuum because she was

(a) One-quarter Q   (b) Half Q
(c) Full Q raised as a human   (d) A Q criminal

167. In "Tapestry," Q showed Picard the life he might have lived. What was Picard's rank in that other life?
(a) Ensign   (b) Lieutenant
(c) Lieutenant commander   (d) Commander

168. In "All Good Things . . ." Q shows Picard the failed beginning of life on what planet?

ARTIFICIAL INTELLIGENCE

169. Who perfected the positronic brain?

170. In "The Measure of a Man," what ruling was made regarding Data?
(a) His right to vote
(b) His right to mate
(c) His right to procreate
(d) His right of self-determination

171. What were the three criteria for sentience cited by Commander Bruce Maddox?

172. The fifth edition of what source states: "An android is an automaton made to resemble a human being"?

173. Which of the following could Data *not* do?
(a) Eat   (b) Have sex   (c) Dream
(d) Use contractions

174. By what name were microscopic robots known?

175. Data once created an android "daughter." Name her.

176. What does her name mean when translated from Hindi?
(a) Beloved   (b) Hope   (c) Wonder   (d) Renewal

177. How many androids in total were known to have been made by Data's creator?
(a) Two   (b) Three   (c) Five   (d) Six

178. Based on what fictional character was a sentient hologram once created by the *Enterprise*-D computer?

179. In "The Quality of Life," the rights of what sentient machines did Data insist on protecting?

180. In the episode "Emergence," what begins to develop a mind of its own?

MISCELLANEOUS DATA

181. In *The Next Generation,* what term is used to describe what was known as a "landing party" in *The Original Series?*

182. Which crew members joined the *Enterprise*-D at Farpoint Station?

183. Who among the following did *not* have some kind of association prior to joining the *Enterprise* crew?
(a) **Riker and Troi** (b) **Picard and Crusher**
(c) **Crusher and Wesley** (d) **Yar and Data**

184. A member of what adversarial species from *The Original Series* served aboard the *Enterprise*-D?

185. Four characters from *The Original Series* appeared in episodes of *The Next Generation.* Three of them were McCoy, Scott, and Spock. Name the fourth.

186. For what previous *Enterprise* captain was an *Enterprise*-D shuttlepod named?

187. In "The Neutral Zone," Data mentioned the year in which the episode took place. It was
(a) **2363** (b) **2364** (c) **2365** (d) **2366**

188. Picard was once arbiter of succession for the leadership of what civilization?
(a) **Klingon** (b) **Romulan** (c) **Cardassian**
(d) **Borg**

189. Which of the following planets was Picard *not* known to have visited?
(a) **Qo'noS** (b) **Romulus** (c) **Cardassia Prime**
(d) **The Borg homeworld**

190. In "Time's Arrow, Part I," which of the following did Data use as stakes during a poker game?
(a) **Gold coins** (b) **His combadge**
(c) **His right hand** (d) **His head**

STAR TREK: THE NEXT GENERATION

191. In which episode of *The Next Generation* did the *Enterprise*-D crew visit Deep Space 9?
- (a) "Unification, Part I"
- (b) "Chain of Command, Part I"
- (c) "Birthright, Part I"
- (d) "Gambit, Part I"

192. In "Lessons," Picard learns that the most accoustically perfect part of the ship is
- (a) The main shuttlebay
- (b) Ten-Forward
- (c) A Jefferies tube intersection
- (d) Stellar cartography

193. In "Schisms," to whom was Data's ode dedicated?

194. In "Thine Own Self," what name was Data given on Barkon IV?

195. True or false: Troi at one time believed she was in love with Picard.

196. In "Yesterday's *Enterprise*," who was the captain of the *Enterprise*-C?
- (a) John Harriman   (b) Rachel Garrett
- (c) Natasha Yar   (d) Montgomery Scott

197. What pre-industrial species believed for a time that Picard was a god?

198. This species was
- (a) Proto-human   (b) Proto-Vulcan
- (c) Proto-Klingon   (d) Proto-Cardassian

199. What three members of the *Enterprise*-D crew have impersonated Romulans?

200. In "Preemptive Strike," with what group was the *Enterprise*-D in conflict?

STAR TREK
DEEP SPACE NINE®

BENJAMIN SISKO

1. Name Sisko's first wife.

2. Name Sisko's second wife.

3. Sisko lost his first wife in battle against
(a) The Tzenkethi (b) The Borg
(c) The Cardassians (d) The Jem'Hadar

4. Whom did Sisko blame personally for the death of his first wife?

5. True or false: Sisko had a brother named Cal.

6. By what title did Sisko become known to the people of Bajor?

7. Who was with Sisko when he discovered the wormhole?
(a) Kira Nerys (b) Miles O'Brien
(c) Julian Bashir (d) Jadzia Dax

8. Who was Sisko's mentor?

9. Which of the following starships did Sisko *not* serve aboard?
(a) *U.S.S. Lexington* (b) *U.S.S. Livingston*
(c) *U.S.S. Okinawa* (d) *U.S.S. Saratoga*

10. What treasured object did Sisko always keep on his desk?

11. Sisko rediscovered a long-lost Bajoran city named
(a) Kendra (b) Opaka (c) B'hala (d) Orbopolis

12. What was Sisko's middle name?

KIRA NERYS

13. While serving aboard Deep Space 9, Kira was an officer in the Bajoran
(a) **Resistance** (b) **Militia** (c) **Special forces**
(d) **Defense ministry**

14. Kira's dual role on Deep Space 9 was first officer and _____ officer.

15. Who was the leader of Kira's resistance cell during the Cardassian occupation of Bajor?

16. In what refugee camp did Kira spend her childhood?
(a) **Singha** (b) **Shakaar** (c) **Dahkur** (d) **Gallitep**

17. In "Second Skin," Kira was kidnapped and surgically altered to look like a member of what species?

18. Name the vedek with whom Kira was once romantically involved.

19. Name the child for whom Kira was the surrogate mother.

20. True or false: In one episode of *Deep Space Nine,* Kira wore a brown Bajoran uniform.

21. To what rank was Kira promoted sometime between the sixth and seventh seasons?

22. In what episode was Kira given a Starfleet commission?

23. What was her rank as a Starfleet officer?

24. Kira disguised herself as a _____ to help Damar and Garak in "What You Leave Behind."

STAR TREK: DEEP SPACE NINE

ODO

25. Where was Odo discovered?
(a) **On Bajor** (b) **On a comet**
(c) **In the Denorios Belt** (d) **In the Badlands**

26. Name the Bajoran scientist who raised Odo.

27. Who first recruited Odo to be chief of security aboard the station?

28. Odo's immediate predecessor as station security chief was
(a) **Damar** (b) **Thrax** (c) **Evek** (d) **Eddington**

29. Although Odo's job was chief of security, by what unofficial title was he affectionately known?

30. What was the full Cardassian name given to Odo when he was being studied in a Bajoran laboratory?

31. What did the name mean?

32. In "Heart of Stone," with whom does Odo confess to being in love?

33. In "The Begotten," Odo tries to raise a baby of what species?
(a) **Jem'Hadar** (b) **Vorta** (c) **Changeling**
(d) **Karemma**

34. True or false: After he was transformed into a "solid," Odo was surgically altered to resemble a Klingon.

35. In "Chimera," Odo said he'd first assumed human shape over how many years ago?
(a) **20** (b) **25** (c) **30** (d) **35**

36. By what organization was Odo infected with a disease designed to kill all changelings?

QUARK

37. Quark was the proprietor of a
  (a) Bar   (b) Gaming establishment
  (c) Holosuite arcade   (d) All of the above

38. In "Ascent," what first edition of Ferengi literature does Quark offer to sell to Odo?

39. What business did Quark once consider taking over at the invitation of his cousin Gaila?
  (a) Weapons merchant   (b) Software manufacturing
  (c) Slave trade   (d) Drug smuggling

40. One of Quark's dreams was to acquire his own
  (a) Marauder   (b) Space station   (c) Moon
  (d) Planet

41. What toys did Ishka save for Quark from his child-hood?

42. Why were they less valuable than they should have been?

43. Who paid for the desiccated remains of Quark in "Body Parts"?

44. Who was Quark's most steady customer?

45. True or false: Quark was once romantically involved with a Cardassian.

46. Quark once married a Klingon. Name her.

47. Who was Quark always calling an idiot?

48. In "Strange Bedfellows," for which missing member of the station crew was Quark pouring a drink every day?

JADZIA DAX

49. Jadzia's people are the Trill. They're known as a _____ species.

50. The sentient life-form within Jadzia is commonly known as a
(a) **Parasite** (b) **Symbiont** (c) **Vermicel** (d) **Slug**

51. Name the captain with the transparent skull whom Jadzia occasionally dated.

52. True or false: Both of Jadzia's parents were joined.

53. Which of the following was Jadzia _not_ known to enjoy?
(a) **Playing _tongo_** (b) **Playing practical jokes**
(c) **Wrestling** (d) **Snacking on tube grubs**

54. What is the name of the Trill initiate assigned to Jadzia in "Playing God"?
(a) **Arjin** (b) **Bareil** (c) **Curzon** (d) **Norvo**

55. Which of the following did Jadzia once describe as "a peculiarity of the Trill"?
(a) **Blue eyes** (b) **Purple blood** (c) **Cold hands**
(d) **An extra row of teeth**

56. What kind of juice did Jadzia like, even though it made her spots itch?
(a) **Prune** (b) **Cranberry** (c) **Icoberry**
(d) **Tulaberry**

57. When she got married, Jadzia became a member of the House of
(a) **Worf** (b) **Mogh** (c) **Martok** (d) **Kang**

58. Who among the following was _not_ interested in Jadzia romantically?
(a) **Jake Sisko** (b) **Julian Bashir** (c) **Quark**
(d) **Worf**

59. True or false: Jadzia was known to have a sister.

60. Who killed Jadzia?

EZRI DAX

61. Before she was joined, Ezri's surname was _____.

62. After being joined, Ezri occasionally got
(a) **Paranoid** (b) **Delusional** (c) **Violent**
(d) **Spacesick**

63. Whom did Sisko ask Ezri to counsel in "Afterimage"?

64. To what rank was Ezri promoted in the same episode?

65. What kind of company did Ezri's family own?
(a) **Transportation** (b) **Terraforming**
(c) **Mining** (d) **Engineering**

66. From which of Dax's former hosts did Ezri seek insight on how to catch a killer?

67. True or false: Ezri had always wanted to be joined.

68. Who on the station crew had the most difficult time adjusting to Ezri as Dax's new host?

69. By what nickname was Ezri known to her brother Norvo?

70. On what starship did Ezri serve before transferring to Deep Space 9?
(a) *U.S.S. Centaur* (b) *U.S.S. Destiny*
(c) *U.S.S. Valiant* (d) *U.S.S. Majestic*

71. With whom did Ezri become romantically involved by the end of the series?

72. In "Tacking into the Wind," what did Ezri say she looked upon with greater skepticism than did Curzon or Jadzia?

STAR TREK: DEEP SPACE NINE

MILES O'BRIEN

73. O'Brien's father hoped Miles would attend the Aldeberan Music Academy to study what instrument?
(a) The trombone   (b) The piano
(c) The cello   (d) The violin

74. In which of the following holosuite programs was O'Brien *not* known to have taken part with Bashir?
(a) Secret agent   (b) The Battle of Britain
(c) The Alamo   (d) The Battle of Gettysburg

75. What bedtime story did O'Brien read to Molly in "If Wishes Were Horses"?

76. Who once replaced O'Brien with a replicant?
(a) The Dominion   (b) The Cardassians
(c) The Argrathi   (d) The Paradas

77. In what episode did a Cardassian scientist believe that O'Brien was attracted to her?

78. What game did O'Brien often play with Bashir in Quark's bar?

79. What was O'Brien's position aboard Deep Space 9?

80. Which unlikely Starfleet cadet did O'Brien take under his wing?

81. How many years of imprisonment did O'Brien experience in "Hard Time"?
(a) 20   (b) 30   (c) 40   (d) 50

82. Who on the station did O'Brien twice visit bearing a gift of bloodwine?

83. True or false: During Kira's pregnancy, there developed some mutual attraction between Kira and O'Brien.

84. At the conclusion of the series, what new assignment did O'Brien accept?

THE DEFINITIVE STAR TREK TRIVIA BOOK

JULIAN BASHIR

85. Bashir graduated _____ in his class from Starfleet Medical.

86. Bashir arrived on Deep Space 9 on the same ship with
(a) Miles O'Brien   (b) Benjamin Sisko
(c) Jadzia Dax   (d) Morn

87. Bashir developed an interest in holosuite programs depicting
(a) Lost causes
(b) Interspecies warfare
(c) Tests of physical endurance
(d) Medical emergencies

88. What resident of the station fed Bashir's appetite for espionage and covert operations?

89. During "In Purgatory's Shadow," it was revealed that Bashir had been kidnapped by the Dominion and interred for over
(a) A week   (b) A month   (c) Five months
(d) A year

90. Name Bashir's teddy bear.

91. What procedure did Bashir's parents force him to undergo as a child?
(a) Cosmetic surgery   (b) Genetic resequencing
(c) Symbiont implantation   (d) Group therapy

92. Name the four genetically enhanced humans with whom Bashir worked in "Statistical Probabilities."

93. In "Inquisition," Bashir was led to believe he was being investigated by what division of Starfleet?

94. Name the friend of Bashir's who created the Vic Fontaine holoprogram.

52

95. On what starship did Bashir travel to Romulus in "Inter Arma Enim Silent Leges"?

    (a) *U.S.S. Intrepid*   (b) *U.S.S. Centaur*

    (c) *U.S.S. T'Kumbra*   (d) *U.S.S. Bellerophon*

96. True or false: Bashir delivered Kirayoshi.

WORF

97. In which episode did Worf join the crew of Deep Space 9?

   (a) "The Way of the Warrior"

   (b) "Apocalypse Rising"

   (c) "Call to Arms"   (d) "Soldiers of the Empire"

98. Early on, Worf disliked having quarters on the station. Where instead did he choose to live?

99. What Klingon icon did Worf find with Jadzia and Kor?

100. Whom did Worf once challenge for command of the Klingon ship *Rotarran?*

101. What was Worf's position aboard Deep Space 9?

102. True or false: Worf's son Alexander used the surname of Worf's foster parents.

103. Worf was a son of _____ but became a member of the House of _____.

104. Name the Klingon weapon Worf began using instead of the more traditional *bat'leth.*

105. In which episode did Worf sacrifice a mission to save his wife's life?

   (a) "The Sacrifice of Angels"

   (b) "Change of Heart"

   (c) "The Sound of Her Voice"

   (d) " 'Til Death Do Us Part"

106. Where was Worf's life pod found in "Penumbra"?

   (a) A dark-matter nebula   (b) A comet field

   (c) The Badlands   (d) The Chin'toka system

107. Whom did Worf fight to the death in "Tacking into the Wind"?

108. What new assignment did Worf accept at the conclusion of the series?

JAKE SISKO

109. The first time Jake appears in "Emissary," he is
(a) Playing baseball   (b) Fishing
(c) Climbing a tree   (d) Writing

110. With whom did Jake become friends shortly after arriving on the station, much to the consternation of the parents of both parties?

111. In "Explorers," what does Jake do reluctantly with his father?
(a) Begin writing
(b) Take a vacation in the Gamma Quadrant
(c) Go sailing in space
(d) Learn to cook

112. In "Progress," how many self-sealing stem bolts did Jake and Nog trade for some *yamok* sauce?
(a) 100 gross   (b) 1,000 gross
(c) 5,000 gross   (d) 10,000 gross

113. What did Jake's girlfriend Mardah do for a living?

114. The woman who seeks out an elderly Jake in "The Visitor" was named
(a) Leah   (b) Korena   (c) Kasidy   (d) Melanie

115. Name Jake's first novel.

116. In "Nor the Battle to the Strong," Jake finds himself on the frontlines of a war between which two civilizations?

117. True or false: Jake's body was once used as the vessel of a Pah-wraith.

118. In "Rapture," Jake authorized surgery to save his father's life at the cost of Sisko's
(a) Visions   (b) Mission   (c) Ship
(d) Status as Emissary

119. In "In the Cards," who was the player featured on the baseball card Jake was trying to obtain?
(a) Jackie Robinson (b) Joe DiMaggio
(c) Willie Mays (d) Hank Aaron

120. What starship manned by Red Squad cadets once rescued Jake and Nog?

RECURRING AND GUEST CHARACTERS

121. Who decided to start a school aboard Deep Space 9?

122. What entity possessed her body in "The Assignment"?

123. What did Kasidy Yates do for a living?

124. What was the name of Yates's ship?
(a) *Xhosa* (b) *Batris* (c) *Nenebek* (d) *Vico*

125. True or false: Yates spent six months in prison.

126. What was Joseph Sisko's profession?
(a) **Preacher** (b) **Politician** (c) **Restaurateur**
(d) **Innkeeper**

127. In what city on Earth did Joseph Sisko live?

128. In "Homefront," to what Starfleet-authorized procedure did Joseph Sisko refuse to submit?
(a) **A telepathic probe** (b) **Blood screening**
(c) **DNA scan** (d) **Interrogation**

129. What was Garak's first name?

130. Name the covert organization that Garak once worked for.

131. Who once made Garak try root beer?
(a) **Julian Bashir** (b) **Jadzia Dax** (c) **Quark**
(d) **Jake Sisko**

132. Who commanded the station during the Cardassian occupation of Bajor?

133. What was his title?
(a) **Governor** (b) **Legate** (c) **Overseer**
(d) **Prefect**

134. What Federation starship was destroyed while transporting him to a hearing?
(a) *U.S.S. Constellation* (b) *U.S.S. Honshu*
(c) *U.S.S. Kornaire* (d) *U.S.S. Farragut*

135. For what job did Rom quit his employment at Quark's?

136. True or false: Before marrying Leeta, Rom had another wife, who left him.

137. When the series ended, what appointment did Rom accept?

138. Name the security officer under Sisko's command who betrayed Starfleet to join the Maquis.

139. What group did this same officer once say was worse than the Borg?
(a) **The Federation**   (b) **The Cardassians**
(c) **The Dominion**   (d) **The Romulans**

140. In "The Sacrifice of Angels," whom did Damar kill before evacuating the station?

141. What vice did Damar frequently exhibit?
(a) **He drank too much.**   (b) **He ate too much.**
(c) **He took drugs.**   (d) **He gambled.**

142. Apart from being a dabo girl at Quark's, Leeta was once described by Bashir as
(a) **An aspiring vedek**   (b) **An amateur sociologist**
(c) **A former gymnast**   (d) **A consummate pilot**

143. Leeta almost left with Dr. Zimmerman to begin a new life on
(a) **Earth**   (b) **The moon**   (c) **Mars**
(d) **Jupiter Station**

144. Who succeeded Kai Opaka as spiritual leader of Bajor?

145. True or false: The new kai sometimes received visions of the Prophets.

146. What Klingon warrior became the supreme commander of the Ninth Fleet?

147. Name the ship he commanded most often.

148. While a prisoner of the Dominion, this warrior sustained injuries that included the loss of
(a) An eye   (b) An ear   (c) Two fingers
(d) A hand

DEEP SPACE 9 AND
THE *U.S.S. DEFIANT*

149. What was the Cardassian name for Deep Space 9?

150. Before it was moved to the mouth of the wormhole, where was the station located?

151. The command center of Deep Space 9 is commonly called _____.

152. The outermost circular section of the station is known as the _____.

153. How many hours make up a day on Deep Space 9?

154. The small interstellar craft assigned to the station are called
(a) **Runabouts**   (b) **Shuttlecraft**
(c) **Shuttlepods**   (d) **Work bees**

155. Which station crew member helped design the *Defiant?*

156. True or false: The *Defiant* is the only Federation starship authorized to use a Klingon cloaking device.

157. The *Defiant* was originally developed as prototype for a class of ship specifically intended to fight and defeat
(a) **The Dominion**   (b) **The Borg**
(c) **The Cardassians**   (d) **The Klingons**

158. In "Defiant," who stole the ship to help the Maquis?
(a) **Michael Eddington**   (b) **Kasidy Yates**
(c) **Chakotay**   (d) **Thomas Riker**

159. What happened to the *Defiant* in "The Changing Face of Evil"?

    (a) It was damaged.

    (b) It was captured.

    (c) It was propelled into the Gamma Quadrant.

    (d) It was destroyed.

160. In "Defiant," what new type of Starfleet ordnance was first seen being used by the *Defiant?*

THE DOMINION

161. In what episode was the Dominion first mentioned?
(a) "The Jem'Hadar"   (b) "The Adversary"
(c) "The Search, Part I"   (d) "Rules of Acquisition"

162. Which of the following names was *not* one by which the rulers of the Dominion are known?
(a) Changelings   (b) Founders   (c) Morphlings
(d) Shape-shifters

163. What Dominion species supervises the Jem'Hadar?

164. Which two Alpha Quadrant species were established to have allied themselves with the Dominion?

165. The disease that the Dominion unleashed on the population of the Teplan system was known as
(a) The phage   (b) The blight   (c) The fever
(d) The plague

166. In what nebula was the Founders' world located before it was destroyed?
(a) Mutara   (b) Omarion   (c) Gamma Erandi
(d) Hugora

167. What two secret organizations conspired to destroy the Founders' homeworld?

168. Whose territory did the Dominion grant to the Breen in exchange for their participation in the war against the Federation?

169. In order to learn about other species in the galaxy, the Founders sent how many infants of their kind into space?

170. Who among the following was *not* known to have been impersonated by a Founder?
(a) Kira   (b) Quark   (c) O'Brien   (d) Bashir

171. During "In the Pale Moonlight," it was revealed that the Dominion had captured what planet within striking distance of Alpha Centauri?

172. True or false: The Dominion used genetic engineering on the Vorta and the Jem'Hadar.

BAJORAN MYSTICISM AND THE PROPHETS

173. By the end of the Cardassian occupation, how many Orbs had been found by the Bajorans?
(a) **Five** (b) **Seven** (c) **Nine** (d) **Ten**

174. The Bajoran Orbs were also known as the "_____ of the Prophets."

175. What was it called when a person experienced the "echo" of an Orb vision?
(a) **Orb echo** (b) **Orb shadow** (c) **Orb reflection**
(d) *pagh'tem'far*

176. Which of the following was *not* known to be an Orb?
(a) **Orb of Prophecy** (b) **Orb of Wisdom**
(c) **Orb of Time** (d) **Orb of Knowledge**

177. Who among the following never looked into an Orb?
(a) **Kira** (b) **Quark** (c) **Jake** (d) **Jadzia Dax**

178. To non-Bajorans, the Prophets are more commonly known as _____ aliens.

179. In which episode did a Prophet use Kira as the vessel for its battle against Kosst Amojan?
(a) **"The Reckoning"** (b) **"The Assignment"**
(c) **"The Sacrifice of Angels"** (d) **"Covenant"**

180. Who were enemies of the Prophets?

181. In which episode was a prophecy describing a "sword of stars" fulfilled by the appearance of a comet?
(a) **"Destiny"** (b) **"Prophet Motive"**
(c) **"Shakaar"** (d) **"The Sword of Kahless"**

182. The Bajoran poet Akorem Laan discovered the celestial temple how many years before Sisko did?
(a) **100** (b) **200** (c) **300** (d) **400**

183. What did the Bajorans call a person's life-force?

184. True or false: The Prophets exist in nonlinear time.

MISCELLANEOUS DATA

185. What "noble hunted" creature did O'Brien befriend in "Captive Pursuit"?

186. In "Dramatis Personae," what device was Sisko compelled to construct?
(a) A clock   (b) A musical instrument
(c) A communicator   (d) A bomb

187. In "Second Sight," what constellation did Sisko and Fenna observe from the station?
(a) The Poet   (b) The Builders
(c) The Runners   (d) The Mariner

188. In "Shadowplay," Odo and Jadzia Dax discovered a colony with a population composed of _____.

189. Which member of the station crew refused to carry a weapon?

190. Who once mistakenly activated an old Cardassian counterinsurgency program?

191. Who was once famous for performing the Cardassian neck trick?
(a) Dukat   (b) Garak   (c) Kira   (d) Odo

192. Who blew up Garak's tailor shop in "Improbable Cause"?

193. In "Apocalypse Rising," who among the following was *not* surgically altered to resemble a Klingon?
(a) Sisko   (b) Odo   (c) Bashir   (d) Miles O'Brien

194. In "Trials and Tribble-ations," which Deep Space 9 crew member lied to Kirk?

195. Before Leeta married Rom, with which station crew member had she been romantically involved?

196. Who helped Odo find the confidence to ask Kira out?

197. Which civilization successfully attacked Starfleet Command on Earth?
(a) Klingons   (b) Jem'Hadar   (c) Cardassians
(d) Breen

198. Which member of the station crew had total recall?
(a) Sisko   (b) Kira   (c) Bashir   (d) Garak

199. Which of Deep Space 9's runabouts was the only one never destroyed?

STAR TREK
VOYAGER®

KATHRYN JANEWAY

1. Janeway's background prior to becoming captain of the *U.S.S. Voyager* was in
(a) **Security** (b) **Engineering** (c) **Sciences**
(d) **Command**

2. In "Coda," whose image did an entity use to convince Janeway that she was dead?

3. With Chakotay's help during a vision quest, what animal did Janeway learn was her spirit guide?

4. On which of the following starships did Janeway serve earlier in her Starfleet career?
(a) *U.S.S. Enterprise* (b) *U.S.S. Tecumseh*
(c) *U.S.S. Okinawa* (d) *U.S.S. Al-Batani*

5. Who wanted Janeway to be the mother of his child?

6. In the altered timeline of the Krenim, what gift from Chakotay did Janeway wear during *Voyager*'s final days?

7. With which *Voyager* crewmate did Janeway once produce offspring?

8. Although Janeway prefers to be addressed as Captain, she once told Harry Kim that _____ would do in a crunch.

9. What did Boothby always leave in Janeway's quarters when she was at the academy?

10. Janeway's dog is named
(a) **Dolly** (b) **Molly** (c) **Sally** (d) **Sadie**

11. According to "Year of Hell," Janeway's birthday is
(a) **April 20** (b) **May 12** (c) **May 20** (d) **June 12**

12. True or false: Janeway lost her husband in a battle against Cardassians.

CHAKOTAY

13. Who sponsored Chakotay's entrance to Starfleet Academy?

14. What did Chakotay build for Janeway as a gift in "Resolutions"?

15. In "Cathexis," what personal belonging of Chakotay's did B'Elanna Torres use to help guide his spirit back to his body?

16. In "Waking Moments," what image did Chakotay use to let himself know when he was dreaming?

17. Chakotay tattooed his forehead in honor of
  (a) His father
  (b) His mother
  (c) His cousins
  (d) His favorite professor at the academy

18. With which Maquis member was Chakotay romantically involved?

19. When Chakotay joined Janeway's crew, he accepted the role of first officer with the rank of _____.

20. Besides Earth, on what planet was Chakotay known to have spent some of his academy training?
  (a) Vulcan   (b) Venus   (c) Mars   (d) Andoria

21. Chakotay failed Professor Vassbinder's class in what subject?
  (a) Transporter theory   (b) Warp propulsion
  (c) Xenobiology   (d) Temporal mechanics

22. Who among the following was *not* a member of Chakotay's Maquis crew when they were flung into the Delta Quadrant?
  (a) Tuvok   (b) Torres   (c) Tom Paris   (d) Seska

23. Chakotay and his father traced their family's heritage back to the _____ People of Central America.

24. True or false: Chakotay's ancestors believed that land was the only thing one could own.

TUVOK

25. What is Tuvok's job on *Voyager?*

26. Name Tuvok's wife.

27. How many children does Tuvok have?

28. At what learning institution did Tuvok teach archery?

29. On which of the following starships is Tuvok *not* known to have served?
(a) *U.S.S. Excelsior*   (b) *U.S.S. Wyoming*
(c) *U.S.S. Saratoga*   (d) *U.S.S. Billings*

30. What Vulcan puzzle did Tuvok teach Kim to play?

31. In "Revulsion," Tuvok was promoted to the rank of
————.

32. True or false: Tuvok was once assigned to Jupiter Station.

33. With what is Tuvok afflicted in "Year of Hell"?
(a) **Paralysis**   (b) **Blindness**   (c) **Deafness**
(d) **Radiation poisoning**

34. What news does Tuvok receive in a letter from home in "Hunters"?

35. What emotion-purging discipline did Tuvok study as a boy?

36. For whom did Tuvok leave a meditation lamp lit in the window of his quarters?

TOM PARIS

37. What is Paris's middle name?

38. Who arranged Paris's release from a Federation penal colony?

39. Where was the colony located?

40. True or false: Prior to his arrival on *Voyager,* Paris had lied to cover up the deaths of three officers.

41. Paris is known for his extraordinary _____ skills.
(a) **Cooking**   (b) **Diving**   (c) **Piloting**
(d) **Diplomatic**

42. What Starfleet rank does Paris's father hold?

43. In the alternate future of "Before and After," whom did Paris marry?

44. What did Paris do for the first time in "The 37's"?

45. Paris's knowledge of _____ came in handy in "Future's End, Parts I and II."
(a) **Twenty-second-century pop culture**
(b) **Twentieth-century pop culture**
(c) **Xenobiology**
(d) **Figure skating**

46. Name the new type of shuttle that Paris conceived.

47. In "Vis à Vis," what kind of car did Paris spend much of the episode in the holodeck working on?

48. True or false: While aboard *Voyager,* Paris was demoted.

B'ELANNA TORRES

49. What is Torres's job aboard *Voyager?*

50. On what planet did Torres grow up?

51. Torres once reprogrammed a Cardassian missile to attack Cardassian targets in the Alpha Quadrant, only to be confronted with it again in the Delta Quadrant. What was the missile's code name?

52. In "Blood Fever," who wanted Torres to become his mate?
(a) Tuvok   (b) Vorik   (c) Paris   (d) Kim

53. Torres dropped out of Starfleet Academy in her
(a) First year   (b) Second year   (c) Third year
(d) Fourth year

54. In the alternate future of "Before and After," what happened to Torres?

55. What shipwide championship did Torres win even though she had a broken ankle?

56. According to Torres, what subject did she nearly fail at the academy?

57. In what episode did Torres first admit her love for Paris?

58. What was Torres's nickname at the academy?

59. What culture did Torres reject throughout her life?

60. True or false: Torres's mother called her 'Lanna.

HARRY KIM

61. Who was Kim engaged to marry before *Voyager* was lost?

62. What is Kim's job on *Voyager?*

63. In "Time and Again," with which two officers did Paris suggest he and Kim double-date?

64. While at the academy, Kim was
   (a) On the swim team
   (b) On the debate team
   (c) In the chess club
   (d) Editor of the academy newspaper

65. Kim has the distinction of having died in two different episodes. Name them.

66. What power did the Clown have over Kim in "The Thaw"?

67. In "Favorite Son," Kim was genetically compelled to go to what planet?

68. Who is Kim's best friend on *Voyager?*

69. True or false: Kim once had a crush on Seven of Nine.

70. Kim's favorite sport is
   (a) Tennis   (b) Parisses squares   (c) Volleyball
   (d) Wrestling

71. In "Scorpion," Kim's body was invaded by biological material from what species?
   (a) Vidiians   (b) Hirogen   (c) 8472   (d) Kazon

72. True or false: Kim once tried dating Torres.

THE DOCTOR

73. The Doctor is the *Voyager* crew's name for the ship's EMH. What does the acronym stand for?

74. Who designed the EMH?

75. Where was the EMH designed?

76. What privilege is the Doctor allowed beginning in "Eye of the Needle"?

77. What name does the Doctor try using in "Heroes and Demons"?

78. Who was the Doctor's first love?

79. What device allows the Doctor to leave the range of the holoemitters in sickbay?

80. The technology behind this device comes from which century?
(a) Twenty-fourth   (b) Twenty-seventh
(c) Twenty-ninth   (d) Thirtieth

81. In "Darkling," which famous poet's personality did the Doctor incorporate into his programming?
(a) Keats   (b) Shelley   (c) Wordsworth   (d) Byron

82. In taking Danara Pel on a date in the holodeck, to what planet did the Doctor go?

83. The Doctor became Seven of Nine's instructor in which of the following subjects?
(a) Ship's systems   (b) Emergency medicine
(c) Human history   (d) Social skills

84. True or false: The Doctor sometimes daydreams that the women aboard *Voyager* are attracted to him.

NEELIX

85. What species is Neelix?

86. Which of the following is *not* one of Neelix's functions aboard *Voyager?*
(a) Cook   (b) Morale officer
(c) Ship's counselor   (d) Goodwill ambassador

87. Who once tried to order a drink from Neelix by addressing him as "bar rodent"?

88. What part of the ship did Neelix convert into a manual kitchen?

89. What was the name of the shipwide broadcast that Neelix used to entertain and enlighten the crew?

90. True or false: Neelix was a Talaxian war hero.

91. With whom was Neelix romantically involved when he joined *Voyager*'s crew?

92. Neelix's familiarity with _____ proved useful when he and Tuvok were stuck on a mag-lev carriage in "Rise."

93. In which episode did Neelix die?

94. From what phobia did Neelix suffer in "Night"?

95. What was Neelix's nickname for Tuvok?

96. Who named a cat after Neelix?

KES

97. What species was Kes?

98. This species ordinarily has a life span of
(a) **Nine years** (b) **19 years** (c) **90 years**
(d) **900 years**

99. How old was Kes when she joined the crew of *Voyager?*

100. With which *Voyager* crew member did Kes train to become an assistant?
(a) **Janeway** (b) **The Doctor** (c) **Paris** (d) **Neelix**

101. Which *Voyager* crew member tutored Kes in controlling her developing psychic abilities?

102. Which of Kes's parents died before she left her homeworld?

103. To whom did Kes donate a lung?
(a) **Neelix** (b) **Torres** (c) **Tuvok** (d) **Paris**

104. Which two members of the crew vied for Kes's romantic attentions?

105. Who was the warlord who transferred his mind into Kes's body?
(a) **Adin** (b) **Demmas** (c) **Resh** (d) **Tieran**

106. The physiological change that makes women of Kes's species ready to conceive a child is known as

_____ .

107. Shortly after joining the crew, into what did Kes convert one of *Voyager*'s cargo bays?

108. As her final gift to *Voyager,* Kes propelled the ship how many thousands of light-years toward the Alpha Quadrant?
(a) **9** (b) **9.5** (c) **10** (d) **10.5**

SEVEN OF NINE

109. What was Seven of Nine's complete Borg designation?

110. What was Seven of Nine's original human name?

111. Where was Seven of Nine born?
(a) Earth   (b) New Providence Colony
(c) Tendara Colony   (d) Wolf 359

112. Seven does not sleep. What does she do instead?

113. As a girl, what was Seven of Nine's favorite color?

114. Whose life did Seven once restore with Borg nanoprobes?
(a) Janeway's   (b) Chakotay's   (c) Torres's
(d) Neelix's

115. The ship in which Seven and her parents made contact with the Borg was named _____.

116. With the help of Kim, what part of the ship did Seven upgrade significantly?
(a) Bridge   (b) Astrometrics lab
(c) Engineering   (d) Sickbay

117. In which episode did Seven spend a month alone while the rest of the crew remained in stasis?
(a) "Thirty Days"   (b) "One"
(c) "Living Witness"   (d) "Course: Oblivion"

118. Who was Seven of Nine's first date?

119. True or false: Seven was grateful to be freed from the Borg collective.

120. What substance allowed Seven the opportunity to explore the Borg concept of perfection?
(a) Dark matter   (b) Omega molecules
(c) Tetryon particles   (d) Boronite

RECURRING AND GUEST CHARACTERS

121. The "Bajoran" Maquis member, Seska, was actually an undercover spy and member of what species?

122. Seska left *Voyager* to join forces with what species?

123. Who was Seska's Maquis informant in the *Voyager* crew?

124. What species was Lon Suder?

125. What was Suder's punishment for killing a fellow crew member?

126. True or false: Suder died trying to lead a mutiny.

127. What type of life-form was the Caretaker?
(a) **Sporocystian** (b) **Carbon** (c) **Silicon**
(d) **Unidentifiable**

128. Name the female Caretaker encountered in "Cold Fire."

129. Name the Ocampa who served her.

130. What starship captain of the twenty-third century did Janeway "meet" in "Flashback"?

131. Janeway once helped a member of the Q achieve his goal of becoming mortal. By what human name did he become known?

132. Ensign Vorik was a member of what species?

133. Name the first child to be born on *Voyager*.

134. What job did her mother have?
(a) **Xenobiologist** (b) **Stellar cartographer**
(c) **Astrophysicist** (d) **Engineer**

135. Name the engineer who, along with Torres, was being considered to become *Voyager*'s new chief engineer after the original was killed.
(a) **Carey** (b) **Hogan** (c) **Seska** (d) **Vorik**

136. Name the twentieth-century human who created an advanced technologies corporation based on the technology of a crashed timeship.

137. What was the name of this man's company?
(a) **Chronowerx** (b) **Chronofax**
(c) **Metatech** (d) **Microdyne**

138. What species was Danara Pel?

139. In "Year of Hell," who was the Krenim commander obsessed with altering time?
(a) **Braxton** (b) **Annorax** (c) **Arturis** (d) **Gegan**

140. What memento of his wife did this man keep encased in glass?

141. In "Unity," who was the Starfleet officer assimilated by the Borg who escaped them and established a new life with other former Borg in the Delta Quadrant?

142. Telek R'Mor was
(a) **A Talaxian gourmet** (b) **A Cardassian doctor**
(c) **A Klingon hero** (d) **A Romulan scientist**

143. Crell Moset was
(a) **A Talaxian gourmet** (b) **A Cardassian doctor**
(c) **A Klingon hero** (d) **A Romulan scientist**

144. What was the full designation given to the Borg that was accidentally created in "Drone"?

THE *U.S.S. VOYAGER*

145. What class of starship is *Voyager?*

146. *Voyager* was catapulted to the Delta Quadrant after entering a region of space known as
(a) The Nekrit Expanse (b) The Krenim Imperium
(c) Fluidic space (d) The Badlands

147. Approximately how many light-years was *Voyager* flung from home?
(a) 50,000 (b) 70,000 (c) 80,000 (d) 90,000

148. What new type of circuitry does *Voyager* use?
(a) Bio-neural (b) Positronic
(c) Quantum-phase (d) Holographic

149. What capability does *Voyager* use for the first time in "The 37's"?

150. When this capability is used, what is *Voyager*'s alert status?
(a) Yellow (b) Red (c) Blue (d) Green

151. What nonstandard type of ordnance does Janeway authorize for use to destroy the Caretaker's Array?
(a) Gravimetric torpedoes
(b) Biomolecular warheads
(c) Chroniton torpedoes
(d) Tricobalt explosives

152. Name the two episodes in which *Voyager*'s warp core is ejected.

153. What visible change occurs to the ship when it goes to warp?
(a) The hull changes color.
(b) The bridge descends into the body of the ship.
(c) The warp nacelles swing upward.
(d) The warp nacelles swing downward.

154. In "Timeless," *Voyager* experiments with what new type of faster-than-light propulsion?
(a) Transwarp   (b) Quantum slipstream
(c) Folded-space transport   (d) Subspace gateway

155. True or false: Since Seven of Nine came aboard, *Voyager* has been using some Borg technology.

156. The crew eventually learned that *Voyager* was not the first Starfleet vessel to be brought to the Delta Quadrant by the Caretaker. The first was the
(a) *U.S.S. Enterprise*-E   (b) *U.S.S. Excelsior*
(c) *U.S.S. Dauntless*   (d) *U.S.S. Equinox*

STAR TREK: VOYAGER

THE DELTA QUADRANT

157. What spatial phenomenon trapped *Voyager* within its event horizon in "Parallax"?
(a) A protomatter nebula   (b) A neutron star
(c) A pulsar   (d) A quantum singularity

158. In what spatial phenomenon did the Komar live?
(a) An inversion nebula   (b) A dark-matter nebula
(c) Fluidic space   (d) Planetary rings

159. In "Deadlock," a spatial scission had what effect on *Voyager* and its crew?

160. True or false: The Voth were an evolved species of dinosaur who left Earth and made their new home in the Delta Quadrant.

161. In "The 37's," how many of *Voyager*'s crew stayed behind on the human colony in the Delta Quadrant?

162. In what episode did the crew find the first direct physical evidence that they were nearing Borg space?
(a) "Basics, Part II"   (b) "Blood Fever"
(c) "Unity"   (d) "Scorpion, Part I"

163. Seven hundred years after *Voyager* passed through their region of the Delta Quadrant, what did the Kyrians and the Vaskans come to believe that Janeway and her crew had done?
(a) Blown up a planet   (b) Started a plague
(c) Started a war   (d) Created life

164. On what Delta Quadrant planet were exact duplicates made of the crew?

165. In "Message in a Bottle," what Delta Quadrant species employed a relay station network that *Voyager* was able to use to establish communication with another Starfleet ship in the Alpha Quadrant?

166. Name the starless region of the Delta Quadrant that is 2,500 light-years across.

167. The region of space that marked the limit of Neelix's knowledge of the Delta Quadrant was called the
(a) Kazon Collective (b) Krenim Imperium
(c) Nekrit Expanse (d) Northwest Passage

168. Which of the following species is *not* native to the Delta Quadrant?
(a) Briori (b) Vidiians (c) Species 8472
(d) Sakari

MISCELLANEOUS DATA

169. Which of the following members of the Maquis was actually a Starfleet officer working undercover?
   (a) Chakotay   (b) Tuvok   (c) Torres   (d) Paris

170. Which continuing character from *Deep Space Nine* made a brief appearance in "Caretaker"?

171. What means for contacting the Alpha Quadrant did *Voyager* discover in "Eye of the Needle"?

172. Who is assigned to train some disorderly Maquis crew members in the finer points of Starfleet protocol and discipline?

173. What three crew members rescue *Voyager* in "Basics, Part II"?

174. Who died saving the ship in this episode?

175. What recurring character died while helping the Kazon try to keep *Voyager?*

176. Which continuing character from *Star Trek: The Next Generation* made a brief appearance in "Death Wish"?

177. In "Flashback," which recurring *Original Series* character was seen as the *Excelsior*'s communications officer?

178. Which two *Voyager* crew members were combined into one being after a transporter accident?

179. What was the new being called?

180. A holosimulation of which recurring character from *The Next Generation* appeared in "Projections"?

181. In "Future's End, Part I," it was revealed that a seismic disaster known as the Hermosa Quake caused the destruction of what major terrestrial city?
   (a) San Diego   (b) Los Angeles   (c) Atlanta   (d) Mexico City

182. Where were Torres and Paris when she admitted her true feelings for him?
(a) **Engineering**   (b) **A holodeck**
(c) **In a shuttlecraft**   (d) **Adrift in space**

183. Name the first two episodes that featured both Seven of Nine and Kes.

184. In "The Killing Game," which terrestrial war was re-created on the holodeck?
(a) **The American Civil War**   (b) **World War I**
(c) **World War II**   (d) **The Korean War**

185. Who was trapped in the holodeck in "Night"?

186. Which continuing character from *The Next Generation* made a brief appearance in "Timeless"?

187. Which *Voyager* crew member was going to show off his juggling skills on Neelix's shipwide talent show?

188. What kind of "currency" sometimes changes hands aboard *Voyager?*
(a) **Latinum**   (b) **Shuttlecraft privileges**
(c) **Holodeck time**   (d) **Replicator rations**

189. Which *Voyager* crew member had been a member of the academy decathlon team?

190. What *Star Trek* movie character reappeared in "Dark Frontier"?

191. In "Random Thoughts," which member of *Voyager's* crew was charged with a capital crime?

192. In "Nemesis," which member of the crew was brainwashed?

193. In "Living Witness," which member of the crew was to stand trial for *Voyager's* "war crimes"?

194. In "Relativity," which member of *Voyager's* crew was recruited for a mission into *Voyager's* past?

195. Name the shuttle in which Paris conducted transwarp experiments in "Threshold."

196. Name the starship that tried to stop Chakotay and Kim in "Timeless."

197. With the medical knowledge of how many cultures was the EMH programmed?
(a) 30   (b) 300   (c) 3,000   (d) 30,000

198. In "The 37's," what relic of the early twentieth century did *Voyager* discover adrift in space?
(a) A typewriter   (b) A bicycle
(c) An automobile   (d) A trolley car

199. In "The Q and the Grey," what rare cosmic event did the *Voyager* crew witness?

200. True or false: In the episode "Deadlock," Harry Kim and the newborn Naomi Wildman died but were replaced by exact duplicates who have been with the ship ever since.

STAR TREK®

THE FILMS

STAR TREK: THE FILMS

THE CREW

1. In *Star Trek: The Motion Picture,* who among these original characters was the only one *not* to have been promoted from his rank in *The Original Series?*
(a) James T. Kirk   (b) Spock   (c) Hikaru Sulu
(d) Pavel Chekov

2. Besides Leonard McCoy, which recurring *Original Series* character was an M.D. in *The Motion Picture?*

3. Which character had grown a beard in *The Motion Picture?*

4. What was Janice Rand's job in *The Motion Picture?*

5. Who had left Starfleet but was brought back to service in *The Motion Picture* via a "reserve activation clause"?

6. In *The Motion Picture,* who left the *U.S.S. Enterprise* without permission in an attempt to contact V'Ger?

7. In *Star Trek II: The Wrath of Khan,* which of the following *Enterprise* crew members is *not* "killed" in the *Kobayashi Maru* simulation?
(a) Kirk   (b) Spock   (c) McCoy   (d) Uhura

8. What is Spock's rank in *The Wrath of Khan?*

9. How many times did Kirk take the *Kobayashi Maru* test?

10. To what medication is Kirk known to be allergic in *The Wrath of Khan?*
(a) Hyronalin   (b) Opthamazine
(c) Retnax V   (d) Occuliron

11. In *The Wrath of Khan,* who was the first officer of the *U.S.S. Reliant?*

12. Which regular character died saving the *Enterprise* in *The Wrath of Khan?*

13. In *Star Trek III: The Search for Spock,* it was revealed that Montgomery Scott always multiplied his repair estimates by a factor of
(a) Two (b) Three (c) Four (d) Five

14. Which recurring character from *The Original Series* made a brief cameo appearance in *The Search for Spock?*
(a) Rand (b) Chapel (c) Kevin Riley (d) Kyle

15. Which of the following Vulcan terms was *not* used in *The Search for Spock?*
(a) *Katra* (b) *Pon farr* (c) *Plak-tow*
(d) *Fal-tor-pan*

16. Who was called "Tiny" in *The Search for Spock?*

17. What was McCoy's father's name?

18. True or false: In *The Search for Spock,* Kirk and his crew steal the *Enterprise.*

19. In *Star Trek IV: The Voyage Home,* who is described as a "quintessential devil"?

20. According to McCoy, who is "not exactly working on all thrusters"?

21. Where was Sulu born?

22. Who said he was from Iowa but worked in outer space?

23. Which of the following was *not* among the crew's tasks in *The Voyage Home?*
(a) Transport whales to the twenty-third century
(b) Restore the correct timeline
(c) Recrystallize dilithium
(d) Keep its ship hidden

24. True or false: Kirk was demoted in *The Voyage Home.*

25. In *Star Trek V: The Final Frontier,* why did Kirk fidget in his seat on the bridge?

26. In *The Final Frontier,* which crew member of the *Enterprise* recognized Sybok?

27. Who is Sybok's father?

28. Who pretended to be captain of the *Enterprise* in *The Final Frontier?*

29. Who helped Kirk, Spock, and McCoy escape from the brig?

30. True or false: Sybok helped Kirk confront his innermost pain.

31. What was Sulu's rank and job during *Star Trek VI: The Undiscovered Country?*

32. In *The Undiscovered Country,* what had Scotty just bought but was called to a meeting before he could enjoy it?
(a) **A boat** (b) **A bottle of Saurian brandy**
(c) **A novel** (d) **A technical journal**

33. Whose photo did Kirk keep in a frame in his quarters in *The Undiscovered Country?*
(a) **The *Enterprise* command staff's**
(b) **Carol Marcus's**
(c) **David Marcus's**
(d) **Abraham Lincoln's**

34. How big a crew did Valeris say was aboard the *Enterprise* in *The Undiscovered Country?*
(a) **300** (b) **400** (c) **430** (d) **500**

35. For what crime were Kirk and McCoy tried and convicted in *The Undiscovered Country?*

36. Who has a difficult time speaking Klingon in *The Undiscovered Country?*

37. Besides Kirk, which two other *Original Series* crew members were featured in *Star Trek Generations?*

38. In *Generations,* the adult child of which *Original Series* crew member served aboard the *Enterprise*-B?

39. In the idyllic fantasy world fashioned within the nexus in *Generations,* with what woman did Kirk get a second chance at happiness?
(a) **Edith Keeler**   (b) **Carol Marcus**
(c) **Antonia**   (d) **Ruth**

40. In *Generations,* which recurring *Next Generation* character was rescued from the *S.S. Lakul?*

41. Which *Next Generation* crew member received a promotion to lieutenant commander in *Generations?*
(a) **Beverly Crusher**   (b) **Deanna Troi**
(c) **Worf**   (d) **Geordi La Forge**

42. In *Generations,* Jean-Luc Picard received word of the death of
(a) **His brother and nephew**   (b) **His sister and niece**
(c) **His niece and nephew**   (d) **His mother and father**

43. In *Star Trek: First Contact,* what physical change had La Forge undergone since he was last seen?

44. Which three officers initiated the *Enterprise*-E's autodestruct sequence in *First Contact?*

45. Who countermanded that autodestruct order?

46. In *First Contact,* who did Picard say is the bravest man he'd ever known?

47. Whom did Picard stay behind to rescue in *First Contact* while the rest of the crew was abandoning ship?

48. True or false: La Forge attended Zefram Cochrane High School.

49. Which two officers chased down a rogue Data during *Star Trek: Insurrection?*

50. In *Insurrection,* what was Data missing after he was reactivated aboard the *Enterprise*-E?
(a) **Several memory engrams** (b) **A subprocessor**
(c) **His left hand** (d) **His left eye**

51. Name the four officers who helped Picard lead the Ba'ku people into the mountains of their planet in *Insurrection.*

52. During *Insurrection,* Data revealed that his legs are how long?
(a) **22 centimeters** (b) **40.0003 centimeters**
(c) **87.2 centimeters** (d) **Exactly one meter**

53. In *Insurrection,* how much shore leave did Picard say he had coming to him?
(a) **Six weeks** (b) **Five months** (c) **214 days**
(d) **318 days**

54. True or false: La Forge's eyes regenerated during *Insurrection.*

FILM CHARACTERS

55. Who was captain of the *Enterprise* at the beginning of *The Motion Picture?*

56. What was the name of the Vulcan science officer assigned to the *Enterprise* at the beginning of *The Motion Picture?*
   (a) Spock (b) Xon (c) Sonak (d) Saavik

57. Who was the new navigator assigned to the *Enterprise* in *The Motion Picture?*

58. What species was the new navigator?

59. By the end of *The Motion Picture,* two of Kirk's officers were no longer part of the crew. How did Kirk instruct Uhura to explain their absence for the record?
   (a) Killed in the line of duty (b) Missing
   (c) On leave (d) Reassigned

60. True or false: V'ger was originally a space probe named *Voyager VII.*

61. In *The Wrath of Khan,* to whom did Spock relinquish command of the *Enterprise* as the ship prepared to leave spacedock?

62. Name the facility where Drs. Carol and David Marcus were stationed in *The Wrath of Khan.*

63. What was David Marcus's relationship to Kirk?

64. Who was the captain of the *U.S.S. Reliant?*

65. While riding a turbolift with Kirk in *The Wrath of Khan,* with what concept did Saavik express difficulty?
   (a) Humor (b) Grief (c) Dishonesty (d) Love

66. During *The Wrath of Khan,* who denied that Kirk was ever a Boy Scout?

67. Name the admiral who conducted an inspection of the *Enterprise* after it returned to spacedock in *The Search for Spock*.

68. Who paid an unexpected visit to Kirk's home in *The Search for Spock?*

69. Name the captain of the *U.S.S. Excelsior* in *The Search for Spock*.

70. The dangerously unstable material used by David Marcus in *The Search for Spock* to make Project Genesis possible was
(a) **Protomatter**   (b) **Antimatter**
(c) **Dark matter**   (d) **Omega molecules**

71. Which two characters in *The Search for Spock* were the first to learn that Spock had regenerated?

72. In *The Search for Spock,* who conducted the "refusion" ritual that restored Spock?
(a) **Saavik**   (b) **Sarek**   (c) **T'Pau**   (d) **T'Lar**

73. Who sent out a planetary distress call in *The Voyage Home?*

74. Which former member of the *Enterprise* crew did *not* join Kirk on the journey back to Earth in *The Voyage Home?*

75. The two whales in *The Voyage Home* were named
(a) **Lucy and Ricky**   (b) **Archie and Edith**
(c) **George and Gracie**   (d) **Will and Grace**

76. Who was Kirk and Spock's tour guide at the Cetacean Institute in *The Voyage Home?*

77. Who was the man in *The Voyage Home* who likely became the inventor of transparent aluminum?
(a) **Dr. Taylor**   (b) **Dr. Nichols**
(c) **Christopher Brynner**   (d) **Henry Starling**

78. In *The Voyage Home,* who admitted that Spock's associates were people of good character?

79. In *The Final Frontier,* who was the Romulan representative to Nimbus III?

80. Who was the Federation representative to Nimbus III?

81. Who was the Klingon consul to Nimbus III?

82. What did Barclay want from Zefram Cochrane in *First Contact?*
(a) His autograph   (b) A photo with him
(c) To shake his hand   (d) A hug

83. In *First Contact,* who was assimilated by the Borg outside the *Enterprise*-E while attempting to stop their modifications of the deflector dish?

84. What did the Ba'ku reject in *Insurrection?*
(a) Technology   (b) War   (c) Hunting   (d) Bathing

85. In *Insurrection,* what skill did Anij admit she hadn't gotten around to yet?
(a) Dancing   (b) Swimming   (c) Painting
(d) Flying a shuttlecraft

86. Which Ba'ku stayed behind in the caves to search for his lost pet in *Insurrection?*

87. In *The Wrath of Khan,* what killed 20 of Khan's followers, including Khan's wife?

88. Name the Klingon commander who wanted the secret of Project Genesis in *The Search for Spock.*

89. Spock refused to shoot Sybok in *The Final Frontier* because
(a) Sybok is Spock's brother.
(b) Sybok is Spock's son.
(c) Sybok once saved Spock's life.
(d) Spock needs Sybok's help.

90. Name the captain of the Klingon bird-of-prey in *The Final Frontier.*

91. Who was the new helmsman of the *Enterprise* in *The Undiscovered Country?*

92. Who continually quoted Shakespeare throughout *The Undiscovered Country?*

93. Who was the leader of the Klingon Empire at the beginning of *The Undiscovered Country?*

94. Who was the leader of the Klingon Empire at the end of *The Undiscovered Country?*

95. Who was the high-ranking Starfleet conspirator against peace with the Klingons?

96. What species was Dr. Tolian Soran?

97. Name Soran's accomplices in *Generations.*

98. Who brought "order to chaos" among the Borg?

99. In *Insurrection,* who claimed to enjoy his skin-stretching sessions?

100. Name the Starfleet officer who allied himself with the Son'a in *Insurrection.*

FILM SHIPS

101. In *The Motion Picture,* what new *Enterprise* bridge station was manned by Chekov?

102. In *The Motion Picture,* what was the name that appeared in English on the hull of the Vulcan shuttle?

103. How many Klingon vessels were destroyed by V'Ger?

104. In *The Wrath of Khan,* what kind of ship was the *Kobayashi Maru?*

105. Terrell and Chekov found cargo carriers from what vessel on Ceti Alpha V?

106. In *The Wrath of Khan,* of what starship did Khan gain control?

107. In *The Search for Spock,* it was revealed that Klingon ships possess what tactical technology previously attributed exclusively to the Romulans?

108. What new ship was introduced in *The Search for Spock* that was supposed to have transwarp drive?

109. In *The Search for Spock,* what science vessel was sent to study the Genesis Planet?

110. Who was captain of that vessel?

111. To initiate the *Enterprise*'s self-destruct sequence, put the following codes in their correct order:
(a) 1B-2B-3   (b) 000 destruct 0   (c) 1-1A-2B
(d) 1-1A

112. What kind of ship did Kirk and crew use to escape the destruction of the Genesis Planet in *The Search for Spock?*

113. In *The Voyage Home,* McCoy painted what name on the hull of the ship that Kirk and crew used to leave Vulcan?

114. What was the first starship to encounter the probe in *The Voyage Home?*

115. What was the name of the nuclear aircraft carrier boarded by Uhura and Chekov in *The Voyage Home?*

116. To what ship did Sulu hope he and his shipmates were assigned at the conclusion of *The Voyage Home?*

117. To what ship were they actually assigned?

118. What two *Enterprise* shuttles were used during *The Final Frontier?*

119. Which of these shuttles crashed onto the *U.S.S. Enterprise*-A hangar deck?

120. True or false: To penetrate the Great Barrier, the *Enterprise*-A was equipped with transwarp drive.

121. Name Gorkon's ship in *The Undiscovered Country.*

122. What was unique about General Chang's bird-of-prey in *The Undiscovered Country?*

123. In *The Undiscovered Country,* what ship was caught by the subspace blast wave resulting from the destruction of Praxis?

124. Which ship tried to distract Chang from attacking the *Enterprise* at Khitomer in *The Undiscovered Country?*

125. Who was the captain of the *U.S.S. Enterprise*-B?

126. In *Generations,* what deck was Kirk on when the *Enterprise*-B suffered a hull breach?

127. Which room in the *U.S.S. Enterprise*-D, featured in *Generations,* was spherical?

128. Which starship was forced to make a course correction in *Generations* because of the destruction of the Amargosa star?

129. In *Generations,* on what modulation were the *Enterprise*-D's shields operating?

130. In *Generations,* on what planet did the *Enterprise*-D saucer section crash-land?

131. Who was at conn when the ship crashed?

132. To what ship did Picard and Riker beam at the end of *Generations?*

133. What new starship was first seen in *First Contact?*

134. What starship did Worf command in *First Contact?*

135. What was the name of Zefram Cochrane's prototype warp ship, seen in *First Contact?*

136. What was this craft built from?

137. In *Insurrection,* what ship did a rogue Data use to attack Ru'afo's ship?
(a) The *Enterprise*-E   (b) The *Defiant*
(c) A shuttlecraft   (d) A scoutship

138. In *Insurrection,* what caused the neutrino emissions coming from the Ba'ku lake?

139. What did the *Enterprise* eject in *Insurrection* in order to seal a subspace tear?

140. What ship did Picard and his team take down to the surface of the Ba'ku planet in *Insurrection?*

MISCELLANEOUS DATA

141. In *The Voyage Home,* who was assigned to convert the cargo hold of a bird-of-prey into a whale tank?

142. How did Kirk get spending money in *The Voyage Home* on twentieth-century Earth?

143. In *The Voyage Home,* where did Kirk see a sign advertising a pair of humpback whales?

144. Where did Scott and McCoy go in *The Voyage Home* to find whale-tank materials?

145. In *The Undiscovered Country,* who opened negotiations with Gorkon at the behest of the Vulcan ambassador?

146. How many Federation assassins boarded Gorkon's ship in *The Undiscovered Country?*

147. For what clue to Gorkon's murder did Spock ask Valeris to search the *Enterprise* in *The Undiscovered Country?*
(a) Two phasers   (b) Two *bat'leths*
(c) Two helmets   (d) Two pairs of gravity boots

148. In *The Undiscovered Country,* who were the two *Enterprise* crew members who killed Chancellor Gorkon?

149. What *Enterprise* crew member coordinated the assassination of Gorkon in *The Undiscovered Country?*

150. The opening shot of *Generations* is
(a) Kirk skydiving
(b) An ocean
(c) Worf being promoted
(d) A champagne bottle tumbling through space

151. In *Generations,* how many survivors did Scott rescue from the *S.S. Lakul* before it was destroyed?

152. In *Generations,* who died preventing the deaths of 230 million people?

153. What are the *Enterprise*-E's orders while the Borg are approaching the Federation border in *First Contact?*

154. What "unites humanity in a way that no one ever thought possible"?

155. How many mag-locks had to be released to set loose the deflector dish in *First Contact?*

156. Who convinced Picard to give the order to abandon ship in *First Contact?*
(a) Worf   (b) Crusher   (c) Troi   (d) Lily Sloane

157. In *Insurrection,* the presence of what substance on the Ba'ku planet prevented transportation?

158. In *Insurrection,* what did the Son'a and the Ba'ku have in common?

159. What familiar foes acquired a new look in *The Motion Picture?*
(a) Klingons   (b) Romulans   (c) Vulcans
(d) Tellarites

160. In *The Motion Picture,* what was the number of the pod that shuttled Kirk to the newly remodeled *Enterprise?*

161. How did Spock travel outside the ship within V'Ger?
(a) In a shuttlecraft   (b) In a shuttlepod
(c) In a runabout   (d) In an EVA suit

162. What kind of communicator was used in *The Motion Picture?*
(a) Handheld   (b) Wrist   (c) Badge
(d) Subcutaneous

163. For what Starfleet order did Kirk tell Scott to prepare in *The Motion Picture?*

164. What heading did Kirk give at the end of *The Motion Picture?*

165. What did Spock give Kirk for his birthday in *The Wrath of Khan?*

166. What did McCoy give Kirk for his birthday in *The Wrath of Khan?*

167. In *The Wrath of Khan,* what was the last life-form indigenous to Ceti Alpha V after the explosion of Ceti Alpha VI?

168. In *The Wrath of Khan,* what code did Spock and Kirk use to mislead Khan about the *Enterprise* repair schedule?
(a) **Days = hours**   (b) **Minutes = hours**
(c) **Weeks = days**   (d) **Days = minutes**

169. What had happened to Kirk's glasses by the end of *The Wrath of Khan?*

170. According to Scott, damage control is easy, but _____ is hard.

171. True or false: Both of Spock's parents appeared in *The Voyage Home.*

172. Who said, "Logic is the cement of our civilization with which we ascend from chaos using reason as our guide"?

173. What was Kiri-kin-tha's First Law of Metaphysics, as quoted by Spock in *The Voyage Home?*

174. What was the one question posed by the computer in *The Voyage Home* that Spock couldn't answer?

175. How much did Kirk get for his glasses in *The Voyage Home?*
(a) $100   (b) $250   (c) $500   (d) $1,000

176. What authors did Kirk cite in *The Voyage Home* as examples of the "giants" of twentieth-century literature?

177. In *The Voyage Home,* what was Kirk's excuse to Dr. Gillian Taylor for Spock's odd behavior?

178. What kind of conveyance did Sulu borrow in *The Voyage Home* to use for transporting material back to the bird-of-prey?
(a) Yacht   (b) Small plane   (c) Bus
(d) Helicopter

179. What mountain did Kirk attempt to climb in *The Final Frontier?*

180. What did Kirk say is the most important reason for climbing a mountain?

181. In *The Final Frontier,* what was forbidden on Nimbus III?
(a) Sex   (b) Loud music
(c) Communication with outsiders   (d) Weapons

182. In *The Final Frontier,* what was the name of the only settlement on Nimbus III?

183. What did the plaque on the antique ship's wheel in the Forward Observation Room of the *Enterprise* in *The Final Frontier* say?

184. In *The Final Frontier,* what experience did Sybok compel Spock to relive?

185. The surface of Rura Penthe, seen in *The Undiscovered Country,* was
(a) An icy wasteland   (b) A desert
(c) A tropical rainforest   (d) Mostly ocean

186. What type of shape-shifter was seen in *The Undiscovered Country?*
(a) Allasomorph   (b) Founders
(c) Changelings   (d) Chameloids

187. Whom did Data push into the water for "fun" in *Generations?*

188. In *Generations,* what did Data "just love scanning for"?

189. How many fatalities were suffered among the crew of the *Enterprise*-D when the ship was destroyed in *Generations?*
(a) **None** (b) **One** (c) **15** (d) **Over 200**

190. What made Data cry at the conclusion of *Generations?*

191. In *Generations,* what did Picard and Riker look for in Picard's ready room after the crash of the *Enterprise*-D?
(a) **Picard's family photo album**
(b) **A Kurlan *naiskos***
(c) **Picard's copy of the collected works of Shakespeare**
(d) **Livingston the lionfish**

192. In the moments before the *Enterprise*-E went back in time in *First Contact* to restore history, how many Borg were detected populating Earth?
(a) **5 billion** (b) **9 billion** (c) **18 billion**
(d) **22 billion**

193. What sounded "Swedish" to Lily in *First Contact?*

194. According to Will Riker in *First Contact,* how many people live on the moon by the twenty-fourth century?

195. What did the Borg hope to accomplish in *First Contact* by modifying the *Enterprise*-E deflector dish?

196. To what literary character did Lily compare Picard in his single-minded quest to destroy the Borg?

197. In *Insurrection,* how many Ba'ku did Ru'afo say were on the planet?

198. What play was Data rehearsing before he left to help study the Ba'ku?

199. Why did Troi say "yuck" when Riker kissed her in *Insurrection?*

200. What kind of weapons were banned by the Khitomer Accords?

SECTION SIX

NEW LIFE AND
NEW CIVILIZATIONS

1. Identify the following species:

(a) _____

(b) _____

(c) _____

(d) _____

(e) _____

(f) _____

(g) _____

(h) _____

(i) _____

(j) _____

(k) _____

(l) _____

NEW LIFE AND NEW CIVILIZATIONS

VULCANS

2. In what episode of *Star Trek: The Original Series* did Sarek first appear?

3. What was Sarek's exact age (in human years) in that episode?
(a) 102.437   (b) 102.347   (c) 103.247   (d) 104.347

4. At what institution did Sarek want Spock to study instead of joining Starfleet?

5. Who was Sarek's first human wife?

6. Who was Sarek's second human wife?

7. Name Sarek's father.

8. Name Sarek's grandfather.

9. With what illness was Sarek afflicted during his final years?
(a) Balt'masor syndrome   (b) Bendii syndrome
(c) Kalla-Nohra syndrome   (d) Irumodic syndrome

10. In what episode of *Star Trek: The Next Generation* did Sarek die?

11. In how many separate *Star Trek* productions (episodes and movies) has Sarek appeared in total?

12. Whom did James T. Kirk once describe as "all of Vulcan in one package"?

13. In what episode of *The Original Series* was the Vulcan mind-meld first shown?

14. Name the two traditional Vulcan weapons Spock used in "Amok Time."

15. How often does an adult Vulcan male experience his "time of mating"?

16. Who aboard the *U.S.S. Voyager* underwent the "time of mating"?

17. What color is Vulcan blood?

18. On what metal is Vulcan hemoglobin based?

19. In a Vulcan body, the heart is located in the same place one would find a human's
(a) **Heart** (b) **Stomach** (c) **Liver** (d) **Left kidney**

20. In "The Savage Curtain," who was described as the father of all that the Vulcans have become?

21. In *Star Trek IV: The Voyage Home,* who was described as the "matron of Vulcan philosophy"?
(a) **T'Lar** (b) **T'plana-Hath** (c) **T'Pau** (d) **T'Pel**

22. What Vulcan technique did Spock use most often to subdue an opponent?

23. True or false: Vulcans have a second, inner eyelid.

24. True or false: In ancient times, Vulcans were emotional and warlike.

25. IDIC, one of the core precepts of Vulcan philosophy, is an English acronym for _____.

26. In *The Next Generation,* what species was said to be similar to the Vulcans in its development but was several hundred years less advanced?
(a) **Romulans** (b) **Breen** (c) **Mintakans**
(d) **Malcorians**

27. Who once said, "Logic is the beginning of wisdom . . . not the end"?
(a) **Spock** (b) **Sarek** (c) **Tuvok** (d) **Vorik**

28. The book of Vulcan philosophy mentioned in the *Star Trek: Voyager* episode "In the Flesh" was entitled
(a) *Order Out of Chaos* (b) *Symmetry of Mind*
(c) *A Cave Beyond Logic* (d) *Shadows and Reflections*

29. According to Spock, the planet Vulcan
(a) **Is overpopulated** (b) **Has two suns**
(c) **Has no moon** (d) **Is growing colder**

30. Match each of the following Vulcan terms with its English description:

(a) *Kal Rekk*	i. A Vulcan puzzle
(b) *Kal-if-fee*	ii. Love at first sight
(c) *Kal-toh*	iii. The blood fever
(d) *Koon-ut-kal-if-fee*	iv. The time of mating
(e) *Kroykah*	v. A method of execution
(f) *Plak-tow*	vi. Marriage or challenge
(g) *Pon farr*	vii. A challenge
(h) *shon-ha'lock*	viii. The command to stop
(i) *tal-shaya*	ix. A Vulcan day of observance

ROMULANS

31. Name the two homeworlds of the Romulan Empire.

32. What is the area dividing the Romulan Empire from the Federation?

33. In "Balance of Terror," Kirk and crew had never seen a Romulan before. They were surprised to find that the Romulans strongly resembled _____.

34. In "Balance of Terror," it was revealed that Earth's war with the Romulans took place
(a) 10 years earlier   (b) 57 years earlier
(c) 100 years earlier   (d) 200 years earlier

35. What device did Kirk steal from a Romulan ship in "The *Enterprise* Incident"?

36. In "The *Enterprise* Incident," what is it about the Romulan ships that startles Montgomery Scott?

37. In the same episode, to whom was the Romulan commander attracted?
(a) Kirk   (b) Spock   (c) Leonard McCoy
(d) Scott

38. What Romulan rule of law did Spock claim when accused of theft on a Romulan ship in "The *Enterprise* Incident"?

39. What beverage of Romulan origin was known to be illegal within the Federation in the twenty-third century?

40. According to Sybok, the place from which creation sprang is known to the Romulans as
(a) *Qui'Tu*   (b) *Vorta Vor*   (c) *Sha Ka Ree*
(d) *Romulus*

41. What treaty established peace between the Romulan Empire and the Federation?

42. This treaty forbids the development of _____ technology by the Federation.

43. Which legendary planet did the captain of the *U.S.S. Yamato* believe was located inside the Romulan Neutral Zone?

44. According to the *Next Generation* episode "The Neutral Zone," how long had it been since the Federation had had any contact with the Romulans?
(a) **Over 28 years**   (b) **Over 53 years**
(c) **Over 75 years**   (d) **Over 100 years**

45. That last contact with the Romulans prior to "The Neutral Zone" was known as
(a) **The Tomed Incident**
(b) **The Battle of Cheron**
(c) **The Norkan massacre**
(d) **The Khitomer massacre**

46. Name the Romulan admiral in "The Defector" who tried to prevent a supposed war between the Romulan Empire and the Federation.

47. On the basis of that admiral's statements, which of the following is *not* a feature of the planet Romulus?
(a) **The Caves of Mak'ala**   (b) **The Valley of Chula**
(c) **Apnex Sea**   (d) **Firefalls of Gal Gath'thong**

48. Which Romulan commander went into Federation space to recover a missing Romulan scoutship in "The Enemy"?

49. Which *Enterprise*-D crew member refused to donate a life-saving infusion to a dying Romulan in "The Enemy"?

50. What Romulan senator betrayed the movement to reunify the Romulans and the Vulcans?

51. True or false: An *Enterprise*-D crewman was one-quarter Romulan.

52. What does a Romulan warbird use as a power source for its warp drive?

53. What did the Romulans do in "Visionary" to try to prevent a Dominion invasion of the Alpha Quadrant?

54. The ruling council of the Romulan Empire is the

_____.

55. The Romulans have a saying: "Never turn your back on a _____."

56. What Romulan senator's death was engineered by Garak to implicate the Dominion?

57. According to Garak, what color is the Romulan heart?

58. At the time of "Inter Arma Enim Silent Leges," who was the Romulan praetor?

59. This character was first seen as a lower official in what episode of *The Next Generation?*

60. Which Romulan made contact with *Voyager* in "Eye of the Needle"?

KLINGONS

61. Who doesn't trust men who smile too much?
(a) Kor (b) Kang (c) Koloth (d) Korax

62. Which Klingon's engine room was once inundated with tribbles?
(a) Kor (b) Kang (c) Koloth (d) Korax

63. Whose ship was destroyed by the *Enterprise?*
(a) Kor (b) Kang (c) Koloth (d) Korax

64. Which Starfleet captain did Kang once face in the Azure Nebula?
(a) Kirk (b) Hikaru Sulu (c) Benjamin Sisko
(d) Kathryn Janeway

65. What enemy infected the children of Kang, Koloth, and Kor with a genetic virus?

66. For whom was Kang's firstborn son named?

67. What battle did Kor once wish to relive in Quark's holosuite?
(a) The Battle of Organia
(b) The Battle of Caleb IV
(c) The Battle of Klach D'Kel Brakt
(d) The Battle of Cheron

68. Name Kang's wife.

69. Which Klingon survived the final assault on the Albino's stronghold?
(a) Kor (b) Kang (c) Koloth (d) Martok

70. Kor once enlisted Jadzia Dax and Worf in a quest to find what Klingon icon?
(a) The Emperor's Crown (b) The Ring of Gorkon
(c) The Sword of Kahless (d) The Grail of Kahless

71. Lursa and B'Etor were the sisters of _____.

72. Lursa and B'Etor's brother had a son. What was his name?

73. *Star Trek VI: The Undiscovered Country* established that the leader of the Klingon High Council is known by the title of
(a) Emperor (b) Chancellor (c) Warlord
(d) *Dahar* Master

74. Who became a figurehead emperor in the *Next Generation* episode "Rightful Heir"?

75. Whom did Gowron succeed as leader of the Klingon Empire?
(a) K'mpec (b) Duras (c) Gorkon (d) Azetbur

76. Against what civilization did Gowron order an attack, believing it had been taken over by the Dominion?

77. What peace accord negotiations did Gowron withdraw from, only to renew them later?

78. Who killed Gowron?

79. In Martok's earliest appearances on *Star Trek: Deep Space Nine,* he was actually a changeling. Name the episode in which the real Martok first appeared.
(a) "The Way of the Warrior, Part I"
(b) "Apocalypse Rising"
(c) "In Purgatory's Shadow"
(d) "By Inferno's Light"

80. Name Martok's wife.

81. Name Martok's son.

82. What Federation attaché turned out to be a Klingon spy in "The Trouble With Tribbles"?
(a) Mr. Lurry (b) Nilz Baris (c) Arne Darvin
(d) Cyrano Jones

83. Kahless was first mentioned in what episode of *The Original Series?*

84. Who gave Kirk a Klingon salute at the end of *The Final Frontier?*

(a) **Klaa**   (b) **Korrd**   (c) **Vixis**   (d) **Spock**

85. What is Praxis?

86. How many years did the Starfleet commander in chief estimate the Klingon Empire had left at the beginning of *The Undiscovered Country?*

87. A Klingon wedding ceremony was first depicted in what episode of *Deep Space Nine?*

88. Worf and friends must endure five trials before his wedding. Four of them are *blood, pain, sacrifice,* and *death.* Name the missing one.

89. Gorkon once declared, "You've not experienced _____ until you've read him in the original Klingon."

90. Which of the following are Klingons known *not* to possess?

(a) **Hearts**   (b) **Ears**   (c) **Taste buds**   (d) **Tear ducts**

91. According to Data in "Yesterday's *Enterprise*," what do the Klingons hold in regard above all else?

92. Which of the following is *not* a Klingon weapon?

(a) *Bat'leth*   (b) *d'k tahg*   (c) **Disruptor**
(d) *Ahn-woon*

93. To warn the afterlife that a Klingon warrior is coming, what do Klingons do when a warrior dies?

94. In which Klingon ceremony do two people bond together to become siblings?

95. *Aktuh and Melota*

(a) **Is a Klingon thrust and parry**
(b) **Is a popular dance**
(c) **Is a Klingon opera**
(d) **Are the names of Worf's grandparents**

96. What is the term for the Klingon tradition that when a warrior dies in battle, his or her comrades stay with the body to keep away the predators and allow the spirit to complete its journey?

97. A great Klingon poet is referred to as a _____ Master.

98. What dish is traditionally served on the Day of Honor?

99. On what ship did Alexander serve in "Sons and Daughters"?
(a) *I.K.S. Rotarran*   (b) *I.K.S. Ya'Vang*
(c) *I.K.S. Ning Tao*   (d) *I.K.S. Klothos*

100. If a Klingon bites you on the cheek, it indicates
(a) **Hunger**
(b) **Hate**
(c) **An invitation to join his or her house**
(d) **Foreplay**

BETAZOIDS

101. What was Lwaxana Troi's full title on Betazed?

102. What did Deanna Troi describe to Lwaxana as a "moldy old pot"?

103. In which episode did a lovestruck Ferengi kidnap Lwaxana?

104. With which scientist did Lwaxana fall in love only to lose him to his society's ritual euthanasia?

105. To whom was Lwaxana engaged in "Cost of Living"?

106. Who was Lwaxana's valet?

107. Whom did Lwaxana marry in "The Muse"?

108. When Lwaxana was last seen on *Deep Space Nine,* she was
(a) Rejuvenated   (b) Pregnant
(c) A widow   (d) Dead

109. What is the Betazoid word for *beloved?*

110. In a Betazoid wedding, the bride traditionally wears
(a) A white dress   (b) A black veil
(c) No shoes   (d) No clothes

111. The typical length of a Betazoid pregnancy is
(a) 8 months   (b) 9 months
(c) 10 months   (d) 11 months

112. What did Lwaxana's valet do during dinner in "Haven" as a traditional means of giving thanks for the food?

113. The ritual telepathic bonding for the preengagement of Betazoid children is called _____.

114. Name the Betazoid whose overdeveloped psychic ability made him shun contact with humanoids.

115. Which among the following species is the only one Betazoids are able to read telepathically?

(a) **Ferengi**   (b) **Human**   (c) **Breen**   (d) **Dopterian**

116. What is the Betazoid relaxation technique that Deanna Troi taught Barclay wherein you tap a nerve behind your ear with two fingers?

117. What stage of a Betazoid woman's life involves quadrupling her sex drive?

118. What virus affects the telepathic abilities of mature Betazoids so that they project their own thoughts onto others?

119. What Betazoid Maquis member was killed protecting *Voyager* from the Kazon?

120. True or false: Betazoids are incapable of interbreeding with other species.

THE BORG

121. In which episode of *The Next Generation* were the Borg introduced?

122. Borg space is located in
(a) **The Alpha Quadrant** (b) **The Beta Quadrant**
(c) **The Gamma Quadrant** (d) **The Delta Quadrant**

123. How do the Borg refer to themselves as a group?

124. A single Borg is referred to as a _____.

125. True or false: A Borg will attack anyone who boards its ship, whether they threaten the Borg or not.

126. To increase their numbers, Borg do not reproduce; instead, they _____.

127. The usual shape of a Borg vessel is
(a) **A tetrahedron** (b) **A cube**
(c) **An octahedron** (d) **A dodecahedron**

128. Borg are
(a) **Shape-shifters** (b) **Cybernetic organisms**
(c) **Holograms**
(d) **Born addicted to a chemical substance**

129. In "I, Borg," what was the designation of the Borg that was rescued by the *Enterprise*-D?

130. What name did Geordi La Forge give that same Borg?

131. Who was the leader of a group of disconnected Borg in "Descent, Part I" and "Descent, Part II"?

132. In *First Contact,* the Borg escape craft had what previously unseen shape?

133. According to Picard in *First Contact,* what is the usual temperature aboard a Borg ship?
(a) **28.4 degrees Celsius** (b) **34.7 degrees Celsius**
(c) **37.2 degrees Celsius** (d) **39.1 degrees Celsius**

134. What quality did the Borg queen note in Picard that she said the Borg sometimes lack?

135. Where was the infamous battle between the Federation and the Borg where the Federation sustained massive casualties, including Sisko's wife?

136. True or false: The Borg are known to have fought the Dominion to a standstill in the distant past.

137. Which *Voyager* crew member was temporarily assimilated by a group of former Borg in "Unity"?

138. With what life-form did the Borg initiate a war that they could end only with *Voyager*'s help?

139. The device in Borg ships that "brings order to chaos" is known as a
(a) **Unimatrix** (b) **Metanexus** (c) **Vinculum**
(d) **Metanode**

140. True or false: In the future depicted in the *Voyager* episode "Relativity," the Borg were shown to be part of the Federation.

FERENGI

141. True or false: Rom almost murdered Quark once.

142. Prinadora was the mother of
(a) **Nog** (b) **Rom** (c) **Zek** (d) **Brunt**

143. In which episode did Rom quit working at Quark's bar and start working for the Bajoran Militia as an engineer?

144. Rom once started a labor union after being inspired by an ancestor of
(a) **Sisko's** (b) **Dr. Julian Bashir's**
(c) **Miles O'Brien's** (d) **Michael Eddington's**

145. With whom did Nog double-date in "Life Support"?

146. Who taught Nog to read when Rom refused to allow the boy to attend school?

147. What was the name of Nog and Jake's bogus company when they were negotiating a land trade in "Progress"?

148. What caused Nog to hide in Vic Fontaine's holoprogram in "It's Only a Paper Moon"?

149. The supreme leader of the Ferengi is known by the title _____.

150. What female Ferengi advised Zek on financial matters?

151. What was Quark and Rom's nickname for their mother?
(a) **Ishkabibble** (b) **Moogie**
(c) **Blessed Exchequer** (d) **Grand Naga**

152. Ishka did many things that embarrassed Quark. Which of the following did she *not* do?
(a) **Wear clothes** (b) **Earn a profit**
(c) **Speak to a male** (d) **Form a union**

153. What was Brunt's job title?

154. In what episode did Brunt first appear?

155. Who was he investigating in that episode?
(a) **Quark** (b) **Rom** (c) **Ishka** (d) **Nog**

156. In what *Next Generation* episode did the Ferengi first appear?

157. What set of rules do the Ferengi live by?

158. How many of these rules are there?

159. What is a Ferengi's preferred form of currency?

160. Name the two Ferengi ordered to investigate the Barzan wormhole who ended up trapped in the Delta Quadrant.

161. What does *FCA* stand for?

162. Who was the first grand nagus?
(a) **Krax** (b) **DaiMon Bok** (c) **Gint** (d) **Zek**

163. Which Ferengi female disguised herself as a male to earn a profit?

164. Ferengi have many different words for *rain*. What word did Quark use to describe the pouring rain on Risa in "Let He Who Is Without Sin . . ."?
(a) *Sleejing* (b) *Glebbening* (c) *Pilthing*
(d) *Florking*

165. According to Quark, there's no word in the Ferengi language for
(a) *Crisp* (b) *Crunchy* (c) *Slimy* (d) *Humid*

166. According to the Ferengi Trade By-Laws, a Ferengi male must purchase _____ from a suitable role model on reaching adulthood.

167. Whom did Nog approach to fulfill this by-law?

168. Which of the following is *not* a component of the Ferengi afterlife?
  (a) The Blessed Exchequer
  (b) The Divine Treasury
  (c) The Abhorred Philanthropist
  (d) The Vault of Eternal Destitution

169. What is the Ferengi homeworld called?

170. Where is the Tower of Commerce located on the Ferengi homeworld?
  (a) The Sacred Marketplace
  (b) Avarice Plaza
  (c) The Commerce District
  (d) The Latinum Intersection

THE DEFINITIVE STAR TREK TRIVIA BOOK

BAJORANS

171. From what Starfleet training program did Ro Laren graduate before joining the Maquis?
(a) **Advanced command training**
(b) **Advanced tactical training**
(c) **Covert operations**
(d) **Operations management**

172. Before she joined the crew of the *Enterprise,* Ro had served aboard the
(a) *U.S.S. Wellington*   (b) *U.S.S. Washington*
(c) *U.S.S. Worthington*   (d) *U.S.S. Lexington*

173. Kai Winn had two known romantic interests during *Deep Space Nine.* Name them.

174. By whom did Winn feel forsaken?

175. What was Winn's given name?

176. What Bajoran sport did Kira Nerys and Vedek Bareil both enjoy playing?

177. Before he became a vedek, Bareil had worked at the monastery as
(a) **A gardener**   (b) **A janitor**
(c) **An office clerk**   (d) **A musician**

178. In which episode did Bashir try to prolong Bareil's life through artificial means?

179. Name the resistance fighter who became first minister of Bajor.

180. Who was the kai who first welcomed Sisko to Bajor and Deep Space 9?

181. What Bajoran terrorist tried to destroy one side of the wormhole to reduce Federation and Cardassian interest in his planet?

182. Of what militant group was this terrorist a member?

183. What Bajoran resistance hero was rescued from a Cardassian labor camp and replaced Kira aboard Deep Space 9?

184. What title was he given along with Kira's job?

185. For whom do the Bajorans hold the greatest reverence?
(a) The kai   (b) The Emissary   (c) The vedek
(d) The First Minister

186. What extremist group tried to overthrow the provisional government to break Bajor away from the Federation and the rest of the galaxy?

187. Who was this group's leader?

188. In the *Deep Space Nine* episode "Collaborator," which two vedeks were the leading contenders to become kai?

189. On Bajor, "the occupation" refers to
(a) One's job
(b) The Dominion invasion
(c) The Cardassian takeover of the planet
(d) The Prophets' guidance of Bajor

190. What was the name of the caste system used on Bajor prior to the occupation?
(a) *Dom-jot*   (b) *Peldor joi*   (c) *D'jarra*   (d) *Duranja*

191. What is the name of Bajor's council of spiritual leaders?

192. What is the annual ceremony during which Bajorans write their troubles on Renewal Scrolls, then burn them to symbolize the end of their problems?

193. What is the name of the Bajoran armed forces?

194. What kind of spacecraft was used by ancient Bajorans that Sisko later re-created to demonstrate how Bajoran travelers could have reached Cardassia over eight centuries earlier?

195. True or false: A Bajoran's surname comes before the given name.

196. True or false: A Founder once tried to cause the Bajoran sun to go nova.

197. How long is a typical Bajoran pregnancy?
(a) **Five months**   (b) **Six months**
(c) **Seven months**   (d) **Eight months**

198. While pregnant, Bajoran women
(a) **Eat a lot**   (b) **Drink a lot**   (c) **Itch a lot**
(d) **Sneeze a lot**

199. According to Sisko, how many Bajorans were killed by the Cardassians during the occupation?
(a) **1 million**   (b) **3 million**   (c) **5 million**
(d) **11 million**

200. The stone spires that marked ancient Bajoran cities' place in the universe were called
(a) *D'jarras*   (b) *Bantacas*   (c) *Duranja*   (d) *Jumja*

CARDASSIANS

201. Who did Gul Dukat blame for the death of his father?

202. To what ruling body was Dukat made military advisor in "The Way of the Warrior"?

203. Name Dukat's half-Bajoran daughter.

204. What was her mother's name?

205. The name of Dukat's freighter in "Return to Grace" was the
(a) *Ravinok* (b) *Groumall* (c) *Galor* (d) *Detapa*

206. True or false: Dukat had an affair with Kira's mother.

207. Dukat once had himself surgically altered to resemble what species?

208. What happened to Dukat when he tried to read the book of the Pah-wraiths?

209. After being exiled to Deep Space 9, what did Garak do to make a living?

210. True or false: Garak once tortured Odo.

211. With whom did Garak often have lunch?

212. Where did Garak once work as a gardener?

213. To whom was Garak attracted, despite being an enemy of her family?

214. In "The Wire," it was learned that Garak had a device implanted in his
(a) Leg (b) Shoulder (c) Head (d) Heart

215. Who was Garak's father?

216. In what episode was Garak affected by a psychotropic drug that induced him to kill several Starfleet personnel?

217. True or false: It was once revealed that Garak was married.

218. Whom did Glinn Damar succeed as leader of Cardassia?

219. In "The Sacrifice of Angels," who does Damar want Dukat to leave behind on the station?

220. In which episode did Damar learn his family had been executed by the Dominion?

221. True or false: After the end of the Dominion war, Damar opened diplomatic relations with the Federation.

222. At which Cardassian settlement did Bashir find Tain in "The Wire"?

223. In what episode did Tain die?

224. Where did he die?

225. Who was known as the Butcher of Gallitep?
(a) **Gul Dukat** (b) **Gul Evek** (c) **Gul Macet**
(d) **Gul Darhe'el**

226. Who had himself surgically altered to look like the Butcher of Gallitep?

227. Name the Cardassian boy adopted by Bajorans as a war orphan.

228. Who was the Cardassian political rebel with whom Quark fell in love?

229. What was the name of the Cardassian group that opposed a peace treaty with Bajor and tried to assassinate the First Minister?

230. Name the futuristic Cardassian novel set during a time of war between the Cardassian and Klingon Empires.

231. What was considered the highest form of literature among the Cardassians?

(a) The epic poem   (b) The repetitive epic

(c) The mythological parody   (d) The heroic tragedy

232. What is the title of the Cardassian work that Garak gave Bashir as an example of this literary form?

233. What Cardassian game did Garak and Nog play in "Empok Nor"?

(a) Kotra   (b) Dabo   (c) Dom-jot   (d) Pyramid

234. What was the motto of the Cardassian Third Battalion?

(a) "Death first."   (b) "Death to all."

(c) "The weak shall perish."   (d) "Blood will flow."

235. Cardassians prefer a climate that is

(a) Arid   (b) Temperate   (c) Arctic   (d) Rainy

TRILLS

236. In what episode of *The Next Generation* were the Trills introduced?

237. What was the name of the Trill in that episode?

238. Name the Trill administrative body responsible for selection of symbiont hosts.

239. What are the candidates for joining called?

240. What is the name for a joined Trill responsible for a candidate's training?
(a) **Master** (b) **Adept** (c) **Observer** (d) **Field docent**

241. Who was responsible for Arjin's initiate training in "Playing God"?

242. The group responsible for caring for the symbionts is known as
(a) **The sentinels** (b) **The guardians**
(c) **The protectors** (d) **The sentries**

243. What is the Trill taboo that prevents the current host from renewing a romance with someone from a previous host's life?

244. True or false: Friendships between joined Trills and members of other species almost always continue into a Trill's next incarnation.

245. What is the Trill ritual where people take on the personalities of former hosts so a current host can "meet" the former hosts?

246. What is the Trill ritual that allows a host to externalize the personality of a previous host?

247. In "Equilibrium," it was revealed that the *official* figure for that fraction of the Trill population suitable for joining is
(a) 1 in 10 (b) 1 in 100 (c) 1 in 1,000
(d) 1 in 10,000

248. In the same episode, it was learned that the *actual* figure is
(a) **One in five**   (b) **One in four**
(c) **One in three**   (d) **One in two**

249. A drop in the level of what chemical can endanger a joined Trill's life?

250. Dr. Lenara Kahn came to Deep Space 9 to study
(a) **Bajor**   (b) **The station's operations**
(c) **The wormhole** (d) **Data on the Gamma Quadrant**

251. In a previous incarnation, the Kahn symbiont had been joined to a woman who was married to one of Dax's previous hosts. What was the name of Kahn's host?

252. Who tried to steal the Dax symbiont in "Invasive Procedures"?

253. Name the Trill bridge officer who served aboard the *Enterprise*-E in *Insurrection*.

254. Symbionts appear to communicate among themselves by way of
(a) **Spoken language**   (b) **Color changes**
(c) **Electrical discharges**   (d) **Telepathy**

255. Trills are more sensitive than most humanoids to
(a) **Heat**   (b) **Cold**   (c) **Light**   (d) **Poison**

VORTA

256. Which of the following Weyoun clones was killed in "To the Death"?

(a) Weyoun Three   (b) Weyoun Four

(c) Weyoun Five   (d) Weyoun Six

257. Which of the following was *not* one of the ways a Weyoun clone met his end?

(a) Transporter accident   (b) Shot by a Ferengi

(c) Shot by Garak   (d) Shot by a Jem'Hadar

258. Which Weyoun was killed when Worf snapped his neck?

(a) Weyoun Four   (b) Weyoun Five

(c) Weyoun Six   (d) Weyoun Seven

259. Who are gods to the Vorta?

260. What unusual powers, never exhibited by any other Vorta, did Eris seem to possess in "The Jem'Hadar"?

(a) Telekinesis   (b) Pyrokinesis   (c) Telepathy

(d) Invisibility

261. What was Kilana's true objective in "The Ship"?

(a) To get back a Dominion ship

(b) To save the life of another Vorta

(c) To save the life of a Jem'Hadar

(d) To save the life of a Founder

262. Who was the Vorta in charge of the internment camp in "By Inferno's Light"?

(a) Eris   (b) Keevan   (c) Deyos   (d) Luaran

263. Name the Vorta who ordered his own men into a trap to save himself in "Rocks and Shoals."

(a) Keevan   (b) Deyos   (c) Yelgrun   (d) Weyoun

264. Name the Vorta whom Kira impersonated in "Tacking into the Wind."

(a) Eris   (b) Luaran   (c) Kilana

(d) Her name was never given.

265. Name the Vorta who agreed to conduct a prisoner exchange on Empok Nor.

(a) Kilana   (b) Eris   (c) Keevan   (d) Yelgrun

JEM'HADAR

266. The genetically engineered Jem'Hadar are dependent on what substance for their survival?
(a) **Metrazene**   (b) **Ermanium**
(c) **Ketracel-white**   (d) *Yamok* **sauce**

267. Who was the only person who could control the adolescent Jem'Hadar aboard Deep Space 9?

268. What Jem'Hadar did Bashir meet in "Hippocratic Oath" who was not born chemically dependent like other Jem'Hadar?

269. According to the Jem'Hadar, _____ brings victory.

270. According to the Jem'Hadar, victory is
(a) **Honor**   (b) **Life**   (c) **Material reward**
(d) **Heavenly reward**

271. The leader among a group of Jem'Hadar is known as
(a) **A commander**   (b) **A first**
(c) **A squadmaster**   (d) **An alpha**

272. According to one of their own people, no Jem'Hadar has ever lived
(a) **25 years**   (b) **30 years**   (c) **35 years**
(d) **40 years**

273. A Jem'Hadar who reaches the age of 20 is known as
(a) **A senior**   (b) **An ancient**   (c) **An immortal**
(d) **An honored elder**

274. Jem'Hadar soldiers can become invisible. The device that makes this possible is called a
(a) **Cloak**   (b) **Veil**   (c) **Shroud**   (d) **Phase**

275. There was friction between the two factions of Jem'Hadar in "One Little Ship." What distinguished the two factions?

FOUNDERS

276. In "The Adversary," a Founder tried to provoke a war between the Federation and the

(a) Klingons (b) Tholians (c) Tzenkethi
(d) Breen

277. In the same episode, the changeling impersonated an ambassador named

(a) Gav (b) Krajensky (c) Kozinski (d) Sloane

278. In "The Die Is Cast," a Founder impersonated

(a) A Cardassian (b) A Romulan
(c) A Vulcan (d) A Klingon

279. In "Broken Link," who was Odo misled to believe was a changeling imposter?

280. With what does the female changeling try to influence Odo?

(a) Latinum
(b) Political power
(c) Evidence of atrocities by "solids"
(d) The lure of the Great Link

281. Who created the disease that affected the changelings during the final months of the war?

282. Who carried that disease to the changelings?

283. What was the name of the changeling Odo met in "Chimera"?

284. Who helped this changeling escape from the detention cell?

285. True or false: If part of a changeling is separated from the main "body," that separated portion reverts to its liquid state.

THE DEFINITIVE STAR TREK TRIVIA BOOK

DELTA QUADRANT LIFE-FORMS

286. What interspecies war caused the development of the metreon cascade?

287. True or false: Neelix never observes the Talaxian custom of sharing the history of a meal before it is consumed.

288. Who was the old friend of Neelix's who was in charge of communications for a Talaxian convoy?
(a) Arixia (b) Paxau (c) Laxeth (d) Wixiban

289. Who was the Talaxian who helped Tom Paris take *Voyager* back from the Kazon in "Basics, Part II"?
(a) Paxim (b) Paxau (c) Wixiban (d) Laxeth

290. Which of Neelix's friends served time in prison on a smuggling charge that Neelix had escaped?
(a) Wixiban (b) Paxim (c) Arixia (d) Paxau

291. What Talaxian location did Neelix re-create as a holoprogram?
(a) Arixia Forest (b) Paxau resort
(c) Prixin Gardens (d) Rinax Island

292. Who was providing for the Ocampa's needs when *Voyager* arrived in the Delta Quadrant?

293. What facility did this provider create to help supply the Ocampa with enough energy to support their entire civilization?
(a) The source (b) The array (c) The matrix
(d) The nexus

294. What civilization tried to steal water and power resources from the Ocampa?

295. Name the Ocampa who encouraged Kes to develop her psychokinetic abilities in "Cold Fire."

296. Which of the following is *not* a Kazon sect?
(a) Pranik (b) Nistrim (c) Pommar (d) Relora

NEW LIFE AND NEW CIVILIZATIONS

297. What technology did the Kazon steal from *Voyager* in "State of Flux"?

298. The Kazon's most valuable ally against *Voyager* was
(a) **Seska** (b) **Suder** (c) **Hogan** (d) **Arturis**

299. Among the Kazon, a sect leader is known as a
(a) **Nagus** (b) **Trabe** (c) **Maje** (d) **Praetor**

300. What species temporarily conquered the Kazon and set the sects to squabbling among themselves?

301. True or false: The Kazon once took control of *Voyager*.

302. What disease ravished the Vidiian species?

303. In one episode, Neelix was captured by desperate Vidiians. Which of his organs did they steal?

304. What is the Vidiian government called?

305. Among the Vidiians, a person whose duty is to find replacement organs for other Vidiians is known as
(a) *Cha'DIch* (b) *Honatta* (c) **Maje** (d) **Gatherer**

306. What did the Vidiians do to B'Elanna Torres in hopes of finding a cure for their affliction?

307. Who succeeded in curing the Vidiians' disease?
(a) **Danara Pel** (b) *Voyager*'s **EMH**
(c) **The think tank** (d) **Seven of Nine**

308. Species 8472 was so named by _____.

309. Which *Voyager* crew member was in telepathic contact with species 8472?

310. What did the Doctor use to counteract the 8472 tissue invading Harry Kim's body?

311. The continuum inhabited by 8472 was called _____ by the *Voyager* crew.

312. How many hours of sleep do members of 8472 require?

313. According to the Doctor in "Someone to Watch Over Me," species 8472 has how many sexes?
(a) One   (b) Three   (c) Five   (d) Six

314. Which Hirogen technology did *Voyager* attempt to use in "Message in a Bottle"?
(a) Weapons   (b) Transporters
(c) Communications relay stations
(d) Food replicators

315. Whom did the Alpha-Hirogen claim as relics of the hunt in "Hunters"?

316. The Hirogen relay station's energy source was a
_____.

317. In "Prey," what were the Hirogen hunting?

318. What did the Hirogen use *Voyager*'s holodeck for in "The Killing Game, Part I" and "The Killing Game, Part II"?

319. Which holographic simulation did they like most?

320. Who are the great polluters of the Delta Quadrant?

321. What type of radiation do their vessels leak?

322. Name the species that brainwashed Chakotay into becoming a soldier against their enemies.

323. Name their enemies.

324. What species employs a gestural language to communicate?
(a) The Tak Tak   (b) The Takarans
(c) The Takrit   (d) Talaxians

HYBRIDS

325. The following characters are all hybrids. Match them to their description.

(a) Spock
(b) Deanna Troi
(c) Simon Tarses
(d) Alexander Rozhenko
(e) Sela
(f) Ba'el
(g) B'Elanna Torres
(h) Neelix
(i) Naomi Wildman

i. Half human, half Klingon
ii. Half human, half Romulan
iii. Seven-eighths Talaxian, one-eighth Mylean
iv. Half human, half Betazoid
v. Half human, half Ktarian
vi. Half human, half Vulcan
vii. Three-quarters human, one-quarter Romulan
viii. Half Klingon, half Romulan
ix. Three-quarters Klingon, one-quarter human

SECTION SEVEN

STARFLEET

$\mathbb{A}$

STARFLEET ACADEMY

1. Where is Starfleet Academy located?

2. Who was Kirk's history teacher at Starfleet Academy?

3. What Klingon's military strategies were required learning when Kirk was a cadet at the academy?

4. Who was the first Vulcan to graduate top of the class at the academy?

5. Name the three people with whom Wesley Crusher competed for a spot at Starfleet Academy in "Coming of Age."

6. Which of the applicants got to go to the academy?

7. Name the professor of creative writing at the academy from whom Jean-Luc Picard and Wesley both took classes.

8. From whom did Picard seek guidance and wisdom while at the academy?

9. What planet is the Academy Flight Range located near?

10. A member of Starfleet Academy's _____ Squadron was killed attempting to perform a dangerous flight stunt.

11. Name the cadet who was killed.

12. Name the stunt the squadron was attempting to perform.

13. In "Tapestry," Picard relived a time in his youth with two of his best friends from the academy. Name the friends.

14. According to Geordi La Forge, "Basic _____ Design" is a required course at the academy.

THE DEFINITIVE STAR TREK TRIVIA BOOK

15. Who was Benjamin Sisko's old academy friend who joined the Maquis?

16. Who was Sisko's Vulcan rival at the academy?

17. Who left Deep Space 9 for a teaching position at Starfleet Academy on Earth in "What You Leave Behind"?

18. Who was Harry Kim's roommate at the academy who helped him with his quantum chemistry class?

19. Which of Kim's academy classmates took his place on *U.S.S. Voyager* in an alternate timeline?

20. Which one of B'Elanna Torres's former professors put a recommendation in her file should she ever wish to return to the academy?

21. In the third year of the academy, there's a six-week program of _____ that Torres missed.

22. What affliction did academy cadets suffer from while training in class-2 shuttles?

23. In "In the Flesh," how long did "Boothby" say he'd been tending the grounds at Starfleet Academy?

24. Name the officers' club at Starfleet Academy.

25. True or false: Nog received two field promotions without needing to complete his academy training.

STARFLEET (GENERAL)

26. Who was the first Vulcan to join Starfleet?

27. The order prohibiting any contact with Talos IV is known as Starfleet General Order
(a) 4   (b) 7   (c) 24   (d) 47

28. Where is Starfleet Headquarters located?

29. What is Starfleet Directive 101?

30. Starfleet General Order 12 refers to
(a) Landing party procedures
(b) Seniority of command
(c) Communications with an approaching vessel
(d) The right to bear arms

31. "No flag officer shall beam into a hazardous area without armed escort" is Starfleet General Order
(a) 12   (b) 15   (c) 18   (d) 46A

32. Which regulation states: "If transmissions are being monitored during battle, no uncoded messages on an open channel"?
(a) 12A   (b) 15A   (c) 18A   (d) 46A

33. Who was the first Klingon in Starfleet?

34. Who was the first android in Starfleet?

35. Who wanted Data declared the property of Starfleet so he could dissect the android?

36. What was the annual Starfleet social function that Picard managed to avoid attending for six years in a row?

37. Who was the first Ferengi in Starfleet?

38. What was the usual method Starfleet employed to test for changeling infiltrators?

39. What division of Starfleet supported Admiral Pressman's efforts to salvage the *U.S.S. Pegasus?*

40. Which *Voyager* crew member informed Starfleet of *Voyager's* situation in "Message in a Bottle"?

THE FEDERATION (GENERAL)

41. The highest law in the Federation prevents interference in other cultures. What was this law known as?

42. Who was the only person to ever turn down a seat on the Federation Council?

43. What was the location of the library containing all the scientific and cultural knowledge from all the planets in the Federation?

44. What Federation body was Picard asked to address in "QPid"?

45. Name the group of former Federation citizens who fought the enforcement of a treaty giving their colonies to the Cardassians.

46. According to Picard in *Star Trek: First Contact,* the Federation has over how many member planets?
(a) 100   (b) 150   (c) 350   (d) 500

47. What political movement decried the moral laxness of Federation citizens in "Let He Who Is Without Sin . . ."?

48. In *Star Trek: Deep Space Nine,* with which of the following civilizations was the Federation *not* at war at some point?
(a) Cardassians   (b) Bajorans   (c) Klingons
(d) The Dominion

49. Name the governing group of the Federation.

50. The office of the Federation president is located in what terrestrial city?

DIPLOMACY

51. What were the delegates assembling to debate in "Journey to Babel"?

52. Members of what species attempted to disrupt this conference?

53. What was the name of the planet used by the Federation for a diplomatic conference in "Lonely Among Us"?

54. Who was the deaf negotiator in "Loud as a Whisper" who taught others to listen?

55. Representatives of what species tried to smuggle an explosive to the Pacifica conference?
(a) **Antedeans** (b) **Anticans** (c) **Barzans**
(d) **Selay**

56. How many Federation legal experts were required to put the treaty together between the Federation and the Sheliak Corporate?
(a) **Between 100 and 200** (b) **Between 200 and 300**
(c) **Between 300 and 400** (d) **Between 400 and 500**

57. Tam Elbrun was brought to the *U.S.S. Enterprise*-D to make first contact with whom?

58. When the host body of Ambassador Odan died, who became temporary host of his symbiont and continued his diplomatic mission?

59. In which episode did Picard need to learn a new way to communicate while trapped on a planet with an alien who spoke exclusively in metaphors?

60. With what species did it take nearly a century for Sarek to conclude negotiations?

61. Who was accused of practicing "cowboy diplomacy"?

62. Vedek Bareil gave his life to negotiate a peace treaty with what species?

COMMAND

63. Match the following captains with their respective birthplaces:

(a) Labarre, France   i. Christopher Pike

(b) Indiana   ii. James T. Kirk

(c) Iowa   iii. Jean-Luc Picard

(d) Mojave   iv. Benjamin Sisko

(e) New Orleans   v. Kathryn Janeway

64. In *Star Trek: The Original Series,* who usurped Kirk's body because she wanted the life and power of a starship captain?

65. What contemporary of Kirk's was the commanding officer of the *Starship Lexington?*

66. Who took command of the *U.S.S. Drake* after Will Riker declined the commission?

67. In "Conspiracy," who asked Picard to meet with him and two other captains without Starfleet's knowledge?

68. In the same episode, whom did Picard say had made captain faster than anyone?

69. Who took command of the *Enterprise*-C after the death of its captain?

70. Which captain was assimilated by the Borg?

(a) Janeway   (b) Picard   (c) Kirk   (d) Sisko

71. Who assigned Jellico to command the *Enterprise*-D in "Chain of Command, Part I"?

72. Who was Riker's captain aboard the *U.S.S. Pegasus?*

73. In which episode was Sisko promoted to captain?

74. Name the captain whose rescue came three years too late in "The Sound of Her Voice."

75. Name the captain of the *U.S.S. Equinox.*

MEDICINE

76. In "The Cage," what did Dr. Boyce prescribe for his weary captain?

77. According to Boyce, what two kinds of customers do both doctors and bartenders get?

78. Who took over running Tantalus V, a penal colony, when its director went insane?

79. Who was the original colony director?

80. Who once said he was beginning to think he could cure a rainy day?

81. Name the doctor who diagnosed Dr. Ira Graves in "The Schizoid Man."

82. Who was known as "The Dancing Doctor"?

83. What did Dr. Katherine Pulaski prescribe for the flu in "The Icarus Factor"?

84. Who developed a vaccine for the Teplan blight?

85. True or false: Bashir developed the cure for the disease that threatened the Founders.

86. Who once referred to himself as "the embodiment of modern medicine"?

87. Who helped the Doctor find a cure for Janeway and Chakotay in "Resolutions"?

88. Who brought the Psi 2000 virus aboard the *Enterprise?*

89. How was the Psi 2000 virus passed along in "The Naked Time" and "The Naked Now"?

90. What substance was the normal treatment for radiation sickness right after the Atomic Age and proved to be the cure for the aging disease that affected the *Enterprise* crew in "The Deadly Years"?

91. What was the substance that replaced the above treatment for radiation sickness by the twenty-third century?

92. Who was the only member of the landing party not to suffer from sudden extreme aging in "The Deadly Years"?

93. In "Journey to Babel," Dr. Leonard McCoy had to perform surgery on Sarek's
(a) **Heart** (b) **Brain** (c) **Liver** (d) **Lungs**

94. In "Amok Time," with what kind of compound did McCoy tell Kirk he was injecting him?

95. With what did McCoy really inject Kirk?

96. What substance did Kirk administer to McCoy, who was suffering from a Vulcan mind meld, in *Star Trek: The Search for Spock?*

97. In *Star Trek: The Voyage Home,* McCoy encountered an elderly woman in a twentieth-century hospital who was undergoing dialysis. He gave her a pill. What did it do?

98. From what did McCoy say Dr. Gillian Taylor was suffering?

99. What does that mean in layperson's terms?

100. What examples of twentieth-century medicine did McCoy call "dealing with medievalism"?

101. What terminal disease was Admiral Mark Jameson suffering from in "Too Short a Season"?

102. What were the Aldeans dying from owing to an ozone leak in the shield surrounding their planet?

103. What medicinal substance were the people of Ornara addicted to in "Symbiosis"?

104. What medical fad seen in the centuries-old survivors in "The Neutral Zone" was no longer practiced in the twenty-fourth century?

105. Who prescribed to Picard ginger tea to cure a cold and steamed milk with nutmeg to cure insomnia?

106. What kind of surgical procedure did a young Picard require after an encounter with some Nausicaans?

107. From what medical condition was Lily Sloane suffering when the *Enterprise*-E crew found her in *First Contact?*

108. What medical solution to a Borg skin problem did the EMH suggest while trying to stall the Borg?

109. What question did Bashir miss on his final exam at Starfleet Medical?

110. What disease is found only in people who were at the Gallitep labor camp?

111. In "Learning Curve," what was the source of the virus afflicting *Voyager*'s bioneural circuitry?

112. What disease developed after exposure to the metreon cascade?

113. What is HTDS?

114. What was unusual about the Delta Quadrant virus contracted by the *Voyager* crew in "Macrocosm"?

115. According to the Doctor, the first rule of _____ is to make sure the patient will live, then move on to the next one.

SCIENCES

116. A Class-M planet is one with
(a) An oxygen–nitrogen atmosphere
(b) No oxygen in its atmosphere
(c) Predominantly nitrogen atmosphere
(d) No atmosphere

117. What did the shape-shifting creature in "The Man Trap" require to survive?

118. From what plant did Professor Robert Crater claim Crewman Darnell died after ingesting?

119. What substance did "Mudd's Women" ingest to maintain their sex appeal?

120. Miners were searching for new deposits of what mineral on Janus VI?

121. What characteristic announced the presence of the dikironium cloud creature in "Obsession"?
(a) Its shadow (b) Moaning
(c) A drop in temperature (d) A sickly-sweet odor

122. What substance did the dikironium cloud creature in "Obsession" feed on?

123. To what were the parasite creatures of Deneva vulnerable?

124. What acted as "happiness pills" on Omicron Ceti III?

125. What substance gave the Platonians their telekinetic abilities?

126. What substance was Elaan's necklace composed of?

127. What material was used to quarantine dangerous life-forms in "Unnatural Selection"?

128. What type of superthin matter was home to the two-dimensional creatures in "The Loss"?

129. In "Starship Mine," what were the terrorists trying to steal?

130. According to Worf in *Star Trek Generations,* trilithium is
   (a) A nuclear inhibitor
   (b) A warp field inhibitor
   (c) Capable of opening a wormhole
   (d) Extradimensional in origin

131. What keeps regenerating the genetic structure of the Ba'ku people?

132. In "Playing God," a universe in its first formative stage, or a _____, was discovered.

133. The Barzan people believed they had discovered the galaxy's first known stable _____.

134. What kind of subatomic particles can be found within the Bajoran wormhole?

135. With what biogenic weapon was Miles O'Brien infected with in "Armageddon Game"?

136. What caused an exact duplicate of *Voyager* to be made in "Deadlock"?

137. What theory proposes that transwarp travel would have the traveler exist everywhere at once?

138. What is the process by which two unrelated species cross to form a separate third species?

139. What class of planet is also known as a Demon-Class planet?

140. In "Night," what type of radiation was detected in the void?

TECHNOLOGY

141. According to Spock, what device is the basis for every important piece of equipment used by Starfleet?

142. Starfleet's standard-issue portable scanning device is called a _____.

143. With what mythical device did Kirk bluff Balok?

144. What structural piece of the *U.S.S. Antares* did Charlie Evans make disappear?

145. What device, intended to soothe the minds of the mentally disturbed, instead drove its creator insane in "Dagger of the Mind"?

146. What object amplified Sylvia and Korob's powers?

147. What object seemed to amplify Trelane's powers?

148. In "Obsession," what did Spock do to the transporter to safely retrieve Kirk?

149. What device provided the Eymorgs with the medical knowledge to remove "Spock's Brain"?

150. Genesis was created as a method of
(a) **Exploration** (b) **Defense** (c) **Propulsion**
(d) **Terraforming**

151. What kind of drive did the *U.S.S. Excelsior* supposedly have?

152. According to Dr. Nichols, how thick would a piece of Plexiglas have to be at 60 feet wide by 10 feet high to withstand the pressure of 18,000 cubic feet of water?

153. When Scott tries talking to the computer and then into the mouse, what does Dr. Nichols suggest he use?

154. What kind of computer did Scott use in Nichols's office?

155. Gillian Taylor thought Kirk's communicator was
(a) A toy   (b) A cell phone   (c) A pager
(d) Annoying

156. How did Spock plan to track Kirk and McCoy on Rura Penthe?

157. What prevented beaming out of Rura Penthe's penal colony?

158. In *Star Trek: The Undiscovered Country,* how did Montgomery Scott suggest the *Enterprise*-B could simulate a torpedo blast to break free from the energy ribbon?

159. What is the machine used to help carry cargo that would otherwise be too heavy or too big for a crew member to move?

160. What device is used so that different species can communicate with one another?

161. What kind of particles are generated in a standard tractor beam?

162. What is the standard medium of data storage used in the twenty-fourth century?

163. Name the force field used to make sure that a person being transported stays within the beam.

164. What is the process by which plasma is injected into the molten core of a planet to reheat it?

165. Name the supercomputer running the Aldeans' planetary systems.

166. In "Time's Arrow," what did the Devidians disguise their neural energy collector as?

167. What kind of artificial structure is a hollow sphere surrounding a sun to harvest the star's total energy output for the people living on the inside of the sphere?

168. What device aboard the *U.S.S. Jenolen* did Scott use to survive while awaiting rescue?

169. What device was used to bring Geordi La Forge and Ro Laren back into phase when they were affected by a Romulan interphase generator?

170. What kind of device allowed Picard and Crusher to read each other's thoughts while on Kesprytt III?

171. What kind of shield technology was developed by Dr. Reyga?

172. What did Picard remove from the Borgified body of Ensign Lynch in *First Contact?*

173. In *First Contact,* into what were the Borg attempting to transform the deflector dish?

174. What obscured the *Enterprise*-E's warp signature so that the ship's passengers were not detected by the Vulcans?

175. What was the malfunction in Data's system in *Star Trek: Insurrection?*

176. What kind of dampening field was used on Orellius to make the use of technology impossible?

177. What weapon of mass destruction was developed by Dr. Ma'Bor Jetrel?

178. What species was the weapon used against?

179. Where was the weapon unleashed?

180. What type of computer chip did Henry Starling's company introduce?

181. What technology did Chakotay and B'Elanna Torres use to ensure that their shuttle would not be detected by twentieth-century Earth's radar?

TRAVELS IN SPACE AND TIME

182. In lieu of spacecraft landings, what do Starfleet officers use to visit a planet after their ship enters orbit?

183. In "Tomorrow Is Yesterday," the *Enterprise* traveled back in time because of a near collision with a _____.

184. In the same episode, a "slingshot maneuver" around the sun was used to return the *Enterprise* to its proper time. In what later episode was this maneuver employed deliberately to revisit the past?

185. In what movie was this maneuver used again?

186. What "machine or being" allowed travel into Earth's past in "City on the Edge of Forever"?

187. What time machine did Kirk, Spock, and McCoy encounter on Sarpeidon that could change someone's cellular structure to match the time period to which he or she traveled?

188. What spatial phenomenon did the *Enterprise* encounter while attempting to achieve warp speed in *Star Trek: The Motion Picture?*

189. According to Picard in *First Contact,* how many light-years wide is the Federation?
(a) 5,000   (b) 8,000   (c) 10,000   (d) 15,000

190. Name the time traveler from the past who traveled to the twenty-fourth century in a stolen time machine.

191. From what century did that time machine originate?
(a) Twenty-second   (b) Twenty-fifth
(c) Twenty-sixth   (d) Twenty-ninth

192. Whose dimensional transportation system did Picard and crew destroy in "Contagion" and Sisko and crew destroy in "To the Death" rather than let hostile forces gain control of the "gateways"?

193. In "Force of Nature," after a subspace rift is found to be caused by excessive warp travel, to what warp factor does the Federation Council limit ships?

194. Whom did Sisko impersonate in "Past Tense, Part I" and "Past Tense, Part II" to preserve the timeline on twenty-first-century Earth?

195. What are the temporal mechanics terms for when someone travels back in time to change history and causes the event that initiated the need to time-travel in the first place?

196. How many temporal violations did Dulmer and Lucsly ascribe to Kirk in "Trials and Tribble-ations"?

197. What method of space travel did the Sikarians employ?

198. Twenty-ninth-century Federation timeships travel by creating artificial _____ rifts.

199. What civilization employs transwarp conduits to travel?

200. In "New Ground," experiments in what revolutionary form of faster-than-light propulsion are conducted by Dr. Ja'Dar with the assistance of the *Enterprise*-D?
(a) Transwarp   (b) Soliton wave
(c) Folded-space transport   (d) Quantum slipstream

ASTROMETRICS

201. How many planets are in the Talos star group?

202. Which one is Class M?

203. What planet was the site of a survey mission where a transporter malfunction created an evil double of Kirk?

204. Where did Christine Chapel find her long-lost fiancé?

205. From what planet was Charlie Evans rescued?

206. Of what planet was Kodos the governor?

207. On what peaceful planet was Scott accused of the murders of two women?

208. Where was the conference scheduled to discuss the admission of the Coridan system into the Federation?

209. On what planet was Teer Akaar leader of the Ten Tribes?

210. What planet did Chekov claim was the site of the murder of his brother Piotr by Klingons, in a sector to which Gowron laid claim a century later?

211. On what planet did Anan 7 declare the *Enterprise* a casualty of a computer-conducted war?

212. In the sky of what planet was the cloud city of Stratos?

213. In the beginning of *Star Trek II: The Wrath of Khan,* the *U.S.S. Reliant* is en route to what planet?

214. Where did the *Enterprise* try to lure the *U.S.S. Reliant* in *The Wrath of Khan?*

215. Where did Spock's casket land in *The Wrath of Khan?*

216. Where does McCoy tell Kirk he must "climb the steps" in *Star Trek III: The Search for Spock?*

217. What planet is known as the "Planet of Galactic Peace"?

218. Where is it located?

219. Where did Kirk, Spock, and McCoy take shore leave in *Star Trek V: The Final Frontier?*

220. Where was the Federation–Klingon peace conference held in *Star Trek VI: The Undiscovered Country?*

221. On what planet is Farpoint Station built?

222. Name the matriarchal planet where four men survived the crash of their freighter only to be treated as fugitives.

223. What legendary peaceful, technologically advanced world had a planetwide cloaking system?

224. Where was the last reported location of the *Enterprise*-C 22 years prior to the *Enterprise*-D's encounter with it?

225. Where did Picard go while on a "Captain's Holiday"?

226. On what planet was La Forge stranded with the recalcitrant Romulan Centurion Bochra?

227. What place did Guinan describe as "like being inside joy"?

228. Into what star did Dr. Tolian Soran first launch a solar probe so he could alter the course of the nexus?

229. Soran tried to adjust the position of what planet so it would pass through the nexus ribbon?

230. Which planet in the Veridian system supported humanoid life?

231. According to Riker in *First Contact,* what three lunar locations can be seen from Earth on a clear day?

232. Within what unstable region of space was the Ba'ku planet located in *Star Trek: Insurrection?*

233. In what region of the Bajoran system is the wormhole located?

234. What is the field of plasma storms near Cardassia that the Bajorans and, later, the Maquis used as a base of operations?

235. What is the fifth moon of Bajor?

236. Where were Martok, Worf, and Bashir imprisoned in "In Purgatory's Shadow" and "By Inferno's Light"?

237. Name the planet colonized by the stranded crew of the *U.S.S. Defiant* in "Children of Time."

238. Where did Bashir's parents take him to have him genetically enhanced?

239. Name the planet where Bashir and Jake Sisko were trapped during a fight between Klingon and Federation forces.

240. What planet did B'Elanna Torres target when she reprogrammed a Cardassian missile?

241. In what nebula did the *U.S.S. Excelsior* face a Klingon task force commanded by Kang?

242. On what planet in the Delta Quadrant do people age backward?

243. In what quadrant would you find the Nekrit Expanse?
(a) Alpha   (b) Beta   (c) Gamma   (d) Delta

STARSHIPS

244. From what ship did the *Enterprise* receive a distress signal in "The Cage"?

245. Name Balok's ship.

246. What ship rescued Charlie Evans from Thasus, only to later be destroyed by him?

247. What ship did Kirk ask to bypass a planned stop so he could offer transport aboard the *Enterprise* to the Karidian Company of Players?

248. On what ship did Kirk serve with Benjamin Finney prior to the *Enterprise?*

249. What starship did Spock sense was destroyed in "The Immunity Syndrome"?

250. What early Federation ship was captured by the supercomputer Landru?

251. What does an NX designation on a ship mean?

252. Name the first ship that Picard commanded.

253. What ship's crew discovered Data after the Crystalline Entity decimated the colony?

254. What was the name of the *Enterprise*-D's sister ship that was infected by a virus that destroyed it in "Contagion"?

255. What ship emerged from the time displacement in "Yesterday's *Enterprise"?*

256. What class of starship was the *U.S.S. Stargazer?*

257. On what ship did O'Brien serve under Captain Benjamin Maxwell?

258. Of what ship was La Forge's mother captain before it was lost?

259. What long-lost ship did the *Enterprise*-D find embedded within asteroid gamma 601 in the Devolin system?

260. What did Riker tell Worf was a "tough little ship"?

261. What ship did Picard as a boy see hundreds of times in the Smithsonian Institution but was unable to touch it?

262. What ship did Thomas Riker steal so he could attack a secret Cardassian military base in the Orias system?

263. What did Quark name the ship given to him in "Little Green Men"?

264. Name Captain Braxton's first timeship.

265. In "Message in a Bottle," what prototype Federation starship used "multivector assault mode"?
(a) *U.S.S. Pegasus*   (b) *U.S.S. Prometheus*
(c) *U.S.S. Dauntless*   (d) *U.S.S. Equinox*

266. "Multivector assault mode" refers to that starship's ability to
(a) **Split into three independent ships**
(b) **Deploy several fighter craft**
(c) **Create holographic decoys of itself**
(d) **Transport assault teams onto enemy spacecraft**

267. Name Captain Braxton's second timeship.

268. What other Federation starship did *Voyager* encounter after several years in the Delta Quadrant?

269. What class of ship was it?

270. Match the ship with its registry:

<table>
<tr><td>

a. *U.S.S. Defiant*
   (*Defiant* class)

b. *U.S.S. Enterprise*
   (*The Original Series*)

c. *U.S.S. Enterprise*-D

d. *U.S.S. Excelsior*

e. *U.S.S. Farragut*
   (*Constitution* class)

f. *U.S.S. Intrepid*
   (*Constitution* class)

g. *U.S.S. Pegasus*

h. *U.S.S. Reliant*

i. *U.S.S. Stargazer*

j. *U.S.S. Voyager*

</td><td>

i. NCC-74656

ii. NCC-1647

iii. NCC-2000

iv. NCC-2893

v. NCC-1864

vi. NCC-1701-D

vii. NX-74205

viii. NCC-1631

ix. NCC-53847

x. NCC-1701

</td></tr>
</table>

271. Match the *Enterprise* with its appropriate class:

<table>
<tr><td>

a. *Enterprise*-A

b. *Enterprise*-B

c. *Enterprise*-C

d. *Enterprise*-D

e. *Enterprise*-E

</td><td>

i. *Galaxy* class

ii. *Sovereign* class

iii. *Excelsior* class

iv. *Constitution* class

v. *Ambassador* class

</td></tr>
</table>

CHRONOLOGY

272. To what year in Earth's history did Kirk, Spock, and McCoy travel in "City on the Edge of Forever"?

273. In what decade did the Eugenics Wars take place?

274. In *Star Trek: The Motion Picture,* how long did Scotty say it had taken to redesign and refit the *Enterprise?*
(a) **Six months** (b) **One year** (c) **18 months**
(d) **Five years**

275. In what year was the *S.S. Botany Bay* launched from Earth?

276. How long was Khan marooned on Ceti Alpha V?

277. How long after Khan's arrival on Ceti Alpha V did Ceti Alpha VI explode?
(a) **A year later** (b) **Six months later**
(c) **Six weeks later** (d) **One week later**

278. What provenance did the pawnshop owner give to Kirk's glasses?

279. By *The Undiscovered Country,* how long had Hikaru Sulu been on his current mission as captain of the *U.S.S. Excelsior?*

280. In *The Undiscovered Country,* how long did McCoy say he'd been ship's surgeon aboard the *Enterprise?*

281. What was the stardate of Kirk's last log entry in *The Undiscovered Country?*

282. How many years passed between the *Enterprise*-B's encounter with the energy ribbon and the *Enterprise*-D's?

283. In *Star Trek Generations,* how many years did Data say he'd been trying to become more human?

284. By the time of *First Contact,* how long had the crew been aboard the *Enterprise*-E?

285. In *First Contact,* to what time period did the *Enterprise*-E travel?

286. What is the exact date to which the *Enterprise*-E traveled back in time?

287. What was the date of Earth's official first contact?

288. For how long did Data say he was tempted by the Borg queen's offer to help him achieve his goal of humanity?

289. How many years prior to *Insurrection* did the Ba'ku leave their homeworld to find a new planet?

290. What historical period is most of "Far Beyond the Stars" set in?

291. In what year were several humans abducted by the Briori and taken to the Delta Quadrant?

COURT OF LAW

292. Who defended Kirk at his court-martial?

293. What was this lawyer's passion?
(a) **Plants** (b) **Books** (c) **Computers**
(d) **Classic cars**

294. Of what crime was Scott accused in "Wolf in the Fold"?

295. What interstellar law did General Chang cite to arrest Kirk and McCoy for the murder of Gorkon?

296. When on trial for Gorkon's murder, who defended Kirk and McCoy?

297. What sentence did the Klingon court pass on Kirk and McCoy for the murder of Gorkon?

298. Whose legal decision determined that Data was a person, not property?

299. What scientist was Will Riker accused of murdering aboard a science station orbiting Tanuga IV?

300. Who was responsible for the death of the scientist?

301. In "The Drumhead," who was on a witch-hunt aboard the *Enterprise*-D in search of conspirators against the Federation?

302. Who was Odo accused of killing in "A Man Alone"?

303. Who was Jadzia Dax trying to protect while accused of murder in "Dax"?

304. In "Necessary Evil," Odo reexamined an unsolved murder that occurred during the occupation. Whom did he discover was involved in the murder?

305. True or false: In the Cardassian justice system, defendants are prejudged guilty and trials are just a formality.

306. In "Tribunal," who was judged guilty of smuggling weapons to be used against the Cardassians?

307. What is the title of an officer of the Cardassian court?

308. Which officer of the Cardassian court counsels the accused but is not supposed to address the court?

309. To where—and for how long—was Thomas Riker sentenced after stealing a ship and attacking the Cardassians in the Orias system?

310. What was Odo's punishment for killing another changeling?

311. What race punishes its criminals by implanting memories of imprisonment in their minds?

312. What was Worf accused of doing in "Rules of Engagement"?

313. Who prosecuted Worf in the same episode?

314. Who defended Worf?

315. What was Tom Paris's punishment after being wrongly convicted of murder on Banea?

316. What were Harry Kim and Tom Paris accused of when they were imprisoned in "The Chute"?

317. What was Torres arrested for in "Random Thoughts"?

SECRET GROUPS

318. Who assigned Lieutenant Commander Dexter Remmick to interrogate the crew of the *Enterprise*-D in "Coming of Age"?

319. Name the Vulcan security agency of which Tallera claimed to be a member in "Gambit, Part I" and "Gambit, Part II."

320. What agency investigated the *U.S.S. Defiant*'s accidental trip to the twenty-third century?

321. Name its agents.

322. With which criminal organization was Quark accused of conspiring in "The Ascent"?

323. When O'Brien was sent to infiltrate the Orion Syndicate, he made friends with ————.

324. When Deanna Troi was surgically altered to resemble a Romulan, she posed as a member of what intelligence service?

325. In "Inter Arma Enim Silent Leges," who was chairperson of the Romulan intelligence group?

326. Who was Sloan's Starfleet accomplice in "Inter Arma Enim Silent Leges"?

327. Who was head of the Obsidian Order when Garak worked for it?

328. Whom did the Obsidian Order kidnap in "Second Skin" so it could expose a legate of being part of a rebellious underground movement?

329. In what system did the Obsidian Order build a fleet of ships?

330. With whom did the Obsidian Order join forces to attack the Founders' homeworld?

331. What organization kidnapped Bashir to try to recruit him?

332. Who was in charge of that recruitment?

ALTERNATE TIMELINES AND PARALLEL UNIVERSES

333. In the alternate universe of "Mirror, Mirror," what characteristic distinguished the alternate Spock from his counterpart?

    (a) A scar   (b) Eye color   (c) A beard

    (d) His accent

334. In the same episode, what was the handheld punishment device used on the alternate *Enterprise?*

335. What device was the key to the alternate Kirk's rise to power?

336. Whom did the alternate Kirk assassinate to become captain of the *Enterprise?*

337. What differentiated the alternate universe of "The Alternative Factor" from our own?

    (a) All its inhabitants were evil.

    (b) The void was white and the stars were black.

    (c) Time flowed in reverse.

    (d) It was made of antimatter.

338. In the alternate timeline of "Yesterday's *Enterprise,*" who was on the *Enterprise* who shouldn't have been?

339. In the same episode, who was missing from the bridge crew?

340. What was Wesley's rank in that episode?

341. With what civilization was the Federation at war in that episode?

342. In the fake future created for Will Riker in "Future Imperfect," who was his first officer?

343. In some of the alternate universes Worf visited in "Parallels," to whom was he married?

344. In "Firstborn," a possible future version of Alexander travels back in time to influence his younger self. By what name did the future Alexander go?

345. In the alternate universe of "Crossover," what two civilizations formed an alliance against Terrans?

346. What was Kira's title in the alternate universe?

347. What was the alternate O'Brien's nickname?

348. What was the alternate Worf's status?

349. In the alternate future of "The Visitor," what was the name of Jake's wife?

350. In the same episode, who eventually became a Starfleet captain?
(a) Bashir   (b) Kira   (c) Nog   (d) Garak

351. According to that episode, who wound up running Quark's bar?

352. In the alternate future of "Children of Time," who was Dax's host?

353. Match the regular characters with their "counter-parts" in "Far Beyond the Stars":
(a) Benny Russell   i. Jadzia Dax
(b) Herbert Rossoff   ii. Martok
(c) Albert Macklin   iii. Benjamin Sisko
(d) Douglas Pabst   iv. Kira Nerys
(e) Kay Eaton   v. Weyoun
(f) Julius Eaton   vi. Jake Sisko
(g) Darlene Kursky   vii. Quark
(h) Jimmy   viii. Miles O'Brien
(i) Preacher   ix. Nog
(j) News Vendor   x. Gul Dukat
(k) Taller Cop   xi. Odo
(l) Shorter Cop   xii. Julian Bashir
(m) Roy Rittenhouse   xiii. Joseph Sisko

354. In the same episode, what magazine did Russell purchase at a newsstand?
(a) *Incredible Tales*   (b) *Fascinating!*   (c) *Galaxy*
(d) *Final Frontier*

355. What *Voyager* crew member detected the temporal disruption in "Time and Again"?
(a) Tuvok   (b) The Doctor   (c) Kes
(d) Seven of Nine

356. In the alternate timeline of "Non Sequitur," which two characters never left Earth to serve on *Voyager?*

357. In the alternate future experienced by Kes in "Before and After," Neelix had become
(a) Captain   (b) A security officer
(c) Operations officer   (d) Flight controller

SECTION EIGHT

PERSONNEL FILES

RELATIVITY

Name the following relatives of the crew:

1. James T. Kirk's son: _____
2. Kirk's brother: _____
3. Kirk's nephew: _____
4. Spock's father: _____
5. Spock's mother: _____
6. Spock's half brother: _____
7. Spock's paternal grandfather: _____
8. Spock's paternal great-grandfather: _____
9. Leonard McCoy's father: _____
10. Hikaru Sulu's daughter: _____
11. Jean-Luc Picard's father: _____
12. Picard's mother: _____
13. Picard's brother: _____
14. Picard's nephew: _____
15. Picard's aunt: _____
16. Will Riker's father: _____
17. Tasha Yar's sister: _____
18. Tasha's daughter (alternate history): _____
19. Beverly Crusher's grandmother: _____
20. Deanna Troi's father: _____
21. Troi's mother: _____
22. Troi's sister: _____
23. Worf's foster father: _____
24. Worf's foster mother: _____

25. Worf's foster brother: _____

26. Worf's father: _____

27. Worf's brother: _____

28. Worf's son: _____

29. Wesley Crusher's father: _____

30. Benjamin Sisko's father: _____

31. Sisko's mother: _____

32. Sisko's sister: _____

33. Jake Sisko's mother: _____

34. Kira Nerys's mother: _____

35. Kira's father: _____

36. Kira's brothers: _____ and _____

37. Julian Bashir's father: _____

38. Bashir's mother: _____

39. Miles O'Brien's daughter: _____

40. O'Brien's son: _____

41. Quark's father: _____

42. Quark's mother: _____

43. Quark's brother: _____

44. Quark's nephew: _____

45. Ezri Dax's mother: _____

46. Ezri's brothers: _____ and _____

47. Chakotay's father: _____

48. Neelix's sister: _____

49. Kes's mother: _____

50. Kes's father: _____

51. Seven of Nine's father: _____

52. Seven of Nine's mother: _____

53. Dax's first host: _____

54. Dax's second host: _____

55. Dax's third host: _____

56. Dax's fourth host: _____

57. Dax's fifth host: _____

58. Dax's sixth host: _____

59. Dax's seventh host: _____

60. Dax's eighth host: _____

61. Dax's ninth host: _____

PETS AND OTHER ANIMALS

62. What was the name of Christopher Pike's horse?

63. When Spock was a child he had a pet
(a) *Targ*   (b) **Horse**   (c) **Parrot**   (d) *Sehlat*

64. Sylvia used a human form to try to seduce Kirk, but what animal form did she take to attack him when he rebuffed her?

65. Name Gary Seven's cat.

66. The Cetacean Institute is the only museum in the world exclusively devoted to
(a) **Marine mammals**   (b) **Pacific sea creatures**
(c) **Dolphins and sharks**   (d) **Whales**

67. Which species of whales did Dr. Gillian Taylor say were virtually gone from Earth's oceans?

68. What creatures did Kirk and crew capture and ride to Paradise City?
(a) **Red horses**   (b) **Large birds**
(c) **Blue unicorns**   (d) **Wild** *targs*

69. What kind of animal appeared to Yar in "Where No One Has Gone Before"?

70. What kind of animal appeared to Worf in "Where No One Has Gone Before"?

71. In "Haven," who had a pet plant that got a little too friendly with Mrs. Miller?

72. What creature from a supposedly extinct species did Kivas Fajo have in his collection of unique items?

73. In "New Ground," what creatures did Alexander Rozhenko try to save from a fire aboard the *U.S.S. Enterprise*-D?

74. What kind of pet was Spot?

75. Who was the only person besides Data who Spot liked?

76. Into what did Spot regress in "Genesis"?

77. What kind of pet was O'Brien's Christina?

78. What kind of animal did Picard keep in his ready room?

79. Name Kirk's dog as seen in *Star Trek Generations.*

80. In which movie did two *Enterprise* captains go horseback riding together?

81. Name the large spiderlike creatures that live on the moons of Bajor.

82. Which recurring Klingon had a pet *targ* that his wife allowed to escape rather than have live in her house?

83. Who was babysitting Kathryn Janeway's dog while she embarked on her mission to find Tuvok in "The Caretaker"?

CREW HOBBIES

84. What board game did Spock often play aboard the *Enterprise* in *Star Trek: The Original Series?*

85. Which of Sulu's hobbies was revealed in "Shore Leave"?
(a) **Xenobotany** (b) **Fencing** (c) **Gun collecting**
(d) **Flying helicopters**

86. Which of the following characters have we *not* seen fencing?
(a) **Sulu** (b) **Picard** (c) **Guinan** (d) **Ezri**

87. Which of the following activities was Data *not* known to do in his quest to understand humanity?
(a) **Writing poetry** (b) **Acting**
(c) **Participating in gymnastics** (d) **Painting**

88. Which *Star Trek: The Next Generation* character was passionate about archaeology?

89. For what mathematical theorem was Picard endeavoring to discover a proof in "The Royale"?

90. To what game did both Riker and Data challenge Sirna Kolrami?

91. Which *Next Generation* character cooked for his crewmates in "Time Squared"?

92. In what childhood hobby did O'Brien and Picard both indulge?

93. What play did Data choose to study/perform to better understand the relationship between a leader and followers in "The Defector"?

94. Who brought "The Game" back to the *Enterprise?*
(a) **Wesley** (b) **Robin Lefler** (c) **Picard**
(d) **Riker**

95. What two people figured out the addictive qualities of "The Game"?

96. What was Sisko's favorite game/pastime?

97. Who thought the Galeo-Manada style of wrestling was a great way to start the day?

98. What card game did Jadzia enjoy playing with Quark?

99. In that game, which of the following was *not* a typical tactic?
(a) **Acquiring** (b) **Confronting** (c) **Giving**
(d) **Evading**

100. What type of ship did Sisko build in "Explorers"?

101. Which *Star Trek: Deep Space Nine* crew member enjoys cooking?

102. What character is fond of singing Klingon opera?
(a) **Worf** (b) **Dax** (c) **Sisko** (d) **Bashir**

103. What advice book was Odo reading in "In Purgatory's Shadow"?

104. Name the game of chance played in Quark's bar on a table similar to a roulette wheel.

105. What game looks like a cross between pool and pinball?

106. Who insisted on putting a dartboard in Quark's bar so they could play?

107. What card game did Quark suggest he and Odo play to pass the time in "The Ascent"?

108. Who built a small-scale model of the Alamo, complete with toy soldiers?

109. What card game did Quark play with Vic Fontaine in "What You Leave Behind"?

110. What game did Paris enjoy playing at Chez Sandrine?

111. In "The Raven," to what hobby did Janeway introduce Seven of Nine?
(a) Tennis **(b) Painting** **(c) Sculpting**
(d) Singing

112. What member of the *U.S.S. Voyager* crew likes to use a holo-imager to take photos of everyone?

FOOD AND DRINK

113. What drink did Balok serve to Kirk, Leonard McCoy, and David Bailey in "The Corbomite Maneuver"?

114. What did Spock throw at Nurse Christine Chapel in "Amok Time"?

115. What meal of Kirk's did tribbles get into?

116. What did Gillian Taylor order for dinner with Kirk?

117. What snack food did Spock provide on the campout in *Star Trek V: The Final Frontier?*

118. In Kirk's note to the galley in *Star Trek VI: The Undiscovered Country,* what is no longer to be served at diplomatic functions?

119. Name the brand and vintage of the champagne used to christen the *Enterprise*-B.

120. What was Picard's favorite tea?

121. What fruit did Riker request from Groppler Zorn in "Encounter at Farpoint" that then suddenly appeared?

122. What drink did Lwaxana Troi offer to make for Dai-Mon Tog while being held aboard his ship?

123. Name Deanna Troi's favorite dessert.

124. What drink did Guinan introduce to Worf in "Yesterday's *Enterprise*" that he declared "a warrior's drink"?

125. How many chocolate sundaes did a mortal Q order in an attempt to assuage his depression?

126. Who spilled hot chocolate on Picard while in engineering?

127. What was one of Dr. Leah Brahms's favorite dishes that Geordi La Forge offered to make for her?

128. Who gave Guinan a bottle of Aldebaran whiskey?

129. What color is Aldebaran whiskey?

130. Who was a cake in Data's dreams?

131. One of Ro Laren's favorite foods was
(a) *Jumja* (b) *Hasperat* (c) *Gagh* (d) **Pizza**

132. What was Data's reaction to the drink Guinan offered him in *Generations?*

133. Klingon coffee is known by the name _____.

134. What was Kira's favorite wine?

135. What was Martok's favorite drink?

136. What do female Ferengi traditionally do to their men's food?
(a) **Cook it** (b) **Avoid touching it**
(c) **Purify it** (d) **Chew it**

137. What food did Jadzia say would add years to Sisko's life?

138. What popular Bajoran snack was sold at stands on the Promenade?

139. *Kanar* is
(a) **A Ferengi drink** (b) **A Cardassian drink**
(c) **A Bajoran drink** (d) **A Trill drink**

140. A popular Cardassian condiment is _____.

141. The little worms Ferengi like to eat are known as _____.

142. What food did Neelix tell Janeway in "The Caretaker" she couldn't live without tasting?

143. What is Janeway's favorite drink?

HOLOPROGRAMS

144. What was the first episode featuring Picard's favorite holonovel character Dixon Hill?

145. Who was Dixon Hill's secretary?

146. When Guinan came to visit Picard in his Dixon Hill holoprogram, what character did she portray?

147. What Sherlock Holmes foil did Data encounter on the holodeck?

148. Who played Watson to Data's Holmes on the holodeck?

149. Whom did Moriarty promise to "fill with tea and crumpets" the next time they met?

150. Name the two episodes in which Moriarty appeared.

151. Name Reginald Barclay's holofantasy version of Deanna Troi in "Hollow Pursuits."

152. Into what simulated society on the holodeck did Lwaxana Troi take Alexander Rozhenko to teach him about joy in "Cost of Living"?

153. Who played sheriff and deputy of the *Ancient West* holoprogram?

154. What town provided the backdrop for the *Ancient West* holoprogram?

155. What role did Deanna Troi play in the *Ancient West* holoprogram?

156. In "Descent, Part I," Data played poker with the holorecreations of which three scientists?

157. In "The Nth Degree," who spent an evening discussing physics with a holo–Albert Einstein?

158. Who liked to travel on the Orient Express on the holodeck?

159. In what holoprogram was Worf's promotion ceremony held in *Generations*?

160. What chapter of "The Big Goodbye" holonovel does Picard first activate in *First Contact*?

161. In *First Contact,* in which chapter of "The Big Goodbye" does Picard find Nicki the Nose?

162. In "Emissary," where did Benjamin Sisko find Jake as they arrived at Deep Space 9?

163. What hologrammatic puzzle that responds to neural theta waves had the Dax symbiont been trying to solve for over a century?

164. What was the name of the criminal mastermind in the secret-agent holoprogram first seen in "Our Man Bashir"?

165. Who punched out Lancelot while playing Guinevere in the holosuite?

166. In the last two seasons of *Star Trek: Deep Space Nine,* what holoprogram location became popular among the station crew?

167. Where and when was this holoprogram set?

168. Who created this holoprogram?

169. Who was the featured character of that holoprogram?

170. Which recurring holoprogram location was introduced in "The Cloud"?

171. Whose program was it?

172. What holosuite simulation did Harry Kim initiate in "Heroes and Demons"?

173. Which *U.S.S. Voyager* crew member has a Victorian-era gothic romance holoprogram?

174. In "Worst Case Scenario," who found a holoprogram about a mutiny aboard *Voyager*?

175. Who wrote this holoprogram?

176. Who rewrote the holoprogram to attack the users?

177. When Janeway wants to take herself out of the twenty-fourth century, which Renaissance-era holo-character does she like to visit?

178. In Tom Paris's holohomage to classic science fiction serials, whom does he portray?

179. What is the name of his archfoe in these serials?

180. Who got to play Queen Arachnia in this program?

MUSIC OF THE SPHERES

181. Match the following musical instruments with their players:

(a) Trombone	i. Kim
(b) Ressikan flute	ii. Data
(c) Bagpipes	iii. Riker
(d) Vulcan lute	iv. Scott
(e) Piano	v. Picard
(f) Clarinet	vi. Spock
(g) Violin	vii. Sisko

182. With what song did Riley torment the crew in "The Naked Time"?

183. What song did Uhura sing in "The Conscience of the King" to cheer up a lonely Kevin Riley?

184. What musical instrument did Trelane insist Uhura play in his drawing room so he could dance?

185. With which member of the *Enterprise* crew did Trelane dance?

186. Who would occasionally accompany Uhura's songs on the lute?

187. Which of the misfits in "The Way to Eden" frequently broke into song?

188. What song did Scott play at Spock's funeral?

189. What song was the punk playing on his boombox on the bus to Sausalito?

190. What song did Kirk and McCoy use for a sing-along in *The Final Frontier?*

191. What tune did Data attempt to whistle in "Encounter at Farpoint"?

192. What tune did Dr. Ira Graves whistle in "The Schizoid Man" in response to Data's expressed wish to become more human?

193. In "11001001," what kind of jazz did Minuet *not* like and why?

194. Q brought a mariachi band aboard the *Enterprise*-D to celebrate what?

195. What song did Riker always have trouble playing and did Troi love to torment him about?

196. What song did Picard encourage the children to sing in "Disaster" to keep their spirits up that he later duets with Neela Daren in "Lessons"?

197. In what episode did Picard receive his flute?

198. What song did O'Brien sing with Benjamin Maxwell, his former captain?

199. Who played the violin for visiting guest Sarek?

200. What was Sarek's reaction to that recital?
(a) He smiled.   (b) He clapped.
(c) He bowed.   (d) He cried.

201. To what composer's work was Picard listening in *First Contact* when Riker reported to him about their patrol?

202. What song was playing on the jukebox when Riker found Deanna Troi and Cochrane in a bar in *First Contact?*

203. To what song did Picard and Lily Sloane dance on the holodeck in *First Contact?*

204. What song did Cochrane play during the launch of the *Phoenix?*

205. What song did Picard and Worf sing to distract Data in *Star Trek: Insurrection?*

206. What type of music did Picard ask the computer to play in his quarters in *Insurrection?*

207. According to Odo, what song did O'Brien like to sing while kayaking in the holosuite?

208. What song was Odo humming after a visit in the holosuite with Vic Fontaine that Benjamin Sisko joined him in singing?

209. What song did Vic and Sisko sing as a duet in "Badda-Bing, Badda-Bang"?

210. What duet from *La Bohème* did the Doctor sing with a fussy opera diva?

211. Tuvok recited part of what Vulcan folk song to soothe the children to sleep in "Innocence"?

212. Name the concerto Harry Kim composed in "Night."

213. What song did the Doctor and Seven of Nine sing in "Someone to Watch Over Me"?

YOUTH

214. What did Charlie Evans give Janice Rand as a gift to impress her?

215. What did Charlie turn three playing cards into?

216. At what game did Spock beat Charlie that made the teenager angry enough to melt the playing pieces?

217. On Miri's planet, what were the children called?

218. On Miri's planet, what were the adults called?

219. What creature attacked the miners of Janus VI to protect its children?

220. In "And the Children Shall Lead," what creature was influencing the orphaned children?

221. Who was the only survivor that the *Enterprise* crew found from Kirk's family in "Operation: Annihilate!"?

222. How many children did the Aldeans kidnap from the *Enterprise* in "When the Bough Breaks"?

223. What passive resistance tactic did Wesley Crusher teach the other kidnapped children in "When the Bough Breaks"?

224. Which little girl reminded Lwaxana Troi of her first daughter?

225. Who was Jake Sisko's best friend?

226. Who baby-sat Kirayoshi O'Brien to prove he was capable of being a successful parent?

227. Of what legendary monster were the children in "Innocence" afraid?

228. Who was the only *Voyager* crew member besides her mother who could get Naomi Wildman to go to sleep?

229. Who tricked Chakotay into thinking he was the father of her child?

SECTION NINE

ABSTRACT KNOWLEDGE

VOICEPRINT IDENTIFICATION

1. "You will be absorbed. Your individuality will merge into the unity of good. And in your submergence into the common being of the Body, you will find contentment, fulfillment. You will experience the absolute good." Who gave this speech?
   (a) The Dominion   (b) The Borg   (c) Vaal
   (d) Landru

2. In "The City on the Edge of Forever," what three words did Kirk tell Edith Keeler would be recommended even over "I love you" in the future?

3. Who told Kirk, "There's no honorable way to kill, no gentle way to destroy; there is nothing good in war except its ending"?

4. According to Uhura, "Cyrano Jones says that _____ is the only love that money can buy."

5. Finish this Klingon proverb that Khan quoted in *Star Trek II: The Wrath of Khan*: "Revenge is a dish _____."

6. About whom did Kirk say, "Of all the souls I have encountered in my travels, his was the most human"?

7. Who said, "The more they overthink the plumbing, the easier it is to stop up the drain"?

8. Who told Picard, "If you were any other man, I would kill you where you stand!"?

9. To whom was McCoy referring when he said, "You treat her like a lady and she'll always bring you home"?

10. Which civilization is known for using the phrase "Resistance is futile"?

11. What Tamarian phrase represents two people coming together as friends by facing a common foe?

12. In "The Icarus Factor," O'Brien notes, "You choose your enemies . . . you choose your friends . . . but ———— . . . that's in the stars."

13. According to Riker in "Data's Day," "Some days you get the bear, and ———— ."

14. Who taught Odo "To become a thing is to know a thing. To assume its form . . . is to begin to understand its existence"?

15. Who gave Sisko the following advice: "There comes a time in every man's life when he must stop thinking and start doing"?
(a) **Curzon Dax** (b) **Jadzia Dax**
(c) **Joseph Sisko** (d) **Jake Sisko**

16. About whom does Rom say, "There's only one person in my life who's always been there for me . . . who's never too busy to listen . . . who reassures me when I'm scared . . . comforts me when I'm sad . . . and who showers me with endless love, without ever asking anything in return"?
(a) **Leeta** (b) **Ishka** (c) **Quark** (d) **Rom**

17. Who said "Truth is usually just an excuse for a lack of imagination"?

18. Who told Douglas Pabst, "You can pulp a story but you cannot destroy an idea"?

19. What does the Doctor often say when activated?

20. Who addresses his spirit guide in the following manner: "A-koo-chee-moya . . . we are far from the sacred places of our grandfathers. We are far from the bones of our people."

21. In "Future's End, Part I," Paris informs Janeway that to fit into the late 20th century culture they would need "Nice clothes, fast car . . . and _____."
(a) a good haircut (b) a cellular phone
(c) lots of attitude (d) lots of money

22. Who asked Janeway "Did anyone ever tell you you're angry when you're beautiful?"

23. According to Seven of Nine in "Hope and Fear," _____ is a word that humans use far too often.

IDENTIFY THE EPISODE

24. In which episode does the *Enterprise* travel back in time to the 1960s just prior to the first moon landing? *The Original Series*

25. An ancient Bajoran ship comes through the wormhole. Its only passenger is a man who claims to be the Emissary of the Prophets. When Benjamin Sisko allows him to assume the power of the Emissary, the man causes chaos among the *D'jarras* of Bajor. *Deep Space Nine*

26. A Founder impersonates an ambassador aboard the *U.S.S. Defiant* to sow dissent among the Alpha Quadrant powers. Odo kills one of his own people. *Deep Space Nine*

27. Jean-Luc Picard skips backward and forward through time, encountering Q and a strange space-time anomaly. The last episode of *The Next Generation*

28. Seven of Nine is left alone with the Doctor as the rest of the crew must remain in stasis during passage through a nebula. *Voyager*

29. Picard is kidnapped and kept in a room with other humanoids so a group of aliens can study the concept of authority. *The Next Generation*

30. Bashir and a group of genetically engineered misfits wreak havoc on the station while trying to find a solution to the war with the Dominion. *Deep Space Nine*

31. Harry Kim falls in love with a holodeck character and asks Tuvok for help in controlling his emotions. Tuvok becomes involved with the holodeck woman only to find she is a proxy for a lonely alien woman. *Voyager*

32. In what episode do the Kazon-Nistrim take over *Voyager* and strand the crew on a planet? *Voyager*

33. A matter and antimatter version of the same man are loose aboard the *U.S.S. Enterprise*. Kirk must trap them both in a corridor between the matter and anti-matter dimensions to prevent them from destroying both universes. *The Original Series.*

34. Spock must return home to Vulcan to mate his be-trothed or die trying, but she has another idea. *The Original Series*

35. The *Enterprise* reaches a colony where the children are the only survivors of a massacre. They appear to have been watched over by a Friendly Angel. *The Original Series*

36. The *Enterprise*-D crew searches for the male sur-vivors of a freighter crash on a matriarchal planet. Will Riker teaches the planet leader about equal rights for men. *The Next Generation*

37. In which episode do Kirk, Montgomery Scott, and McCoy rapidly age? *The Original Series*

38. The *Enterprise* crew encounters an innocent people still living in paradise thanks to the benevolence of a god named Vaal. When the crew brings knowledge of other ways into paradise, Vaal gets angry. *The Original Series*

39. Kirk is forced to prove his resourcefulness to a pow-erful race of aliens who trap him on a planet in a fight to the death against the lizardlike captain of a Gorn ship. He impresses them with the advanced quality of mercy. *The Original Series*

40. Julian Bashir and O'Brien are hunted by a people whose biological weapons they just helped to destroy. Keiko O'Brien is told of their deaths. *Deep Space Nine*

41. The *Enterprise*-D finds a planet that is one big weapons showroom and it has their ship as its practice target and a holographic salesman who won't take no for an answer. *The Next Generation*

42. While escorting Quark to a Federation Grand Jury hearing, Odo and Quark are forced to crash-land on a barely habitable planet and must rely on each other to survive until help can arrive. *Deep Space Nine*

43. Keiko is possessed by the spirit of a fallen Prophet. O'Brien enlists Rom's help to make the modifications the life-form demands to keep Keiko alive. *Deep Space Nine*

44. Kes moves backward in time from old age to conception. *Voyager*

45. Picard and Beverly Crusher must escape an extremist political group while telepathically linked by a device. *The Next Generation*

46. A virus initially created during the Cardassian occupation is passed through the food replicators aboard Deep Space 9, making everyone unable to communicate with one other. *Deep Space Nine*

47. A dog clears Tom Paris of a murder charge. *Voyager*

48. The Doctor tampers with his hologrammatic matrix to introduce a little excitement into his personality and the result is deadly. *Voyager*

49. In an attempt to strengthen its position in the Delta Quadrant, the *U.S.S. Voyager* tries to ally itself with various factions of the Kazon Collective, but the Kazon use the opportunity for treachery. *Voyager*

50. A blind woman is the only possible ambassador to a species whose appearance makes human beings go mad. *The Original Series*

51. A woman trades bodies with Kirk so she can captain a starship. *The Original Series*

52. Worf pines for a Klingon woman while helping Quark court her. Dax finally gets Worf's attention. *Deep Space Nine*

53. Picard helps resolve Data's status as a person, not property, in a trial judged by Picard's old flame. *The Next Generation*

54. While Spock and Leonard McCoy are trapped in an Ice Age with a beautiful woman, James T. Kirk is put on trial for witchcraft and no one can find the way back to the library-like time travel repository. *The Original Series*

55. The *Enterprise* travels back in time to the 1960s, where it intercepts a transgalactic transporter beam containing a man. He claims to be an Earthling raised by aliens who's returned to save the planet. However, Kirk, Spock, and the stranger's hip young—but clueless—secretary keep getting in the way of his (and his cat's) effort to complete their mission. *The Original Series*

56. Q wants Kathryn Janeway to be the mother of his child. *Voyager*

57. The crew travels back in time when Data's head is discovered in some old Earth ruins. Mark Twain visits the ship. *The Next Generation*

58. Spock cries. Hikaru Sulu fences. Kevin Riley sings. And it's all the fault of a virus invading the ship. *The Original Series*

59. Sisko, Worf, Odo, and Miles O'Brien infiltrate a Klingon stronghold to expose Gowron as a changeling. But General Martok has other ideas. *Deep Space Nine*

60. A Jem'Hadar baby is found that grows into a teenager at an extraordinary rate. Odo tries to teach it not to be a fighter. *Deep Space Nine*

61. Which episode is an allegory for the Vietnam War, with two factions supporting opposite sides in a war in which neither belongs? *The Original Series*

62. In what episode does a boy choose to emulate Data and "be" an android rather than deal with the loss of his parents? *The Next Generation*

63. In what episode is the murderer a dog—or rather an organism that takes the shape of a dog? *The Next Generation*

64. In which episode do Geordi La Forge and Ro Laren believe they are ghosts? *The Next Generation*

65. In what episode does Kai Opaka die but is then brought back to life? *Deep Space Nine*

66. In which episode does an alien virus invade the Deep Space 9 computer systems, become attached to O'Brien's company, and refuse to leave? *Deep Space Nine*

67. The scientist who first studied Odo comes to the station to help Odo hunt down another shape-shifter that is loose on the station. *Deep Space Nine*

EPISODE TITLES

How well do you know your episode titles? Identify the series to which each title belongs:

(a) *The Original Series*   (b) *The Next Generation*
(c) *Deep Space Nine*   (d) *Voyager*

68. "Accession"

69. "Afterimage"

70. "Allegiance"

71. "Alliances"

72. "Arena"

73. "Attached"

74. "Babel"

75. "Bliss"

76. "Bloodlines"

77. "Cathexis"

78. "Catspaw"

79. "Chimera"

80. "Chrysalis"

81. "Clues"

82. "Coda"

83. "Conspiracy"

84. "Contagion"

85. "Conundrum"

86. "Counterpoint"

87. "Covenant"

88. "Crossfire"

89. "Crossover"

116. "Juggernaut"

117. "Justice"

118. "Legacy"

119. "Lessons"

120. "Liaisons"

121. "Lifesigns"

122. "Macrocosm"

123. "Maneuvers"

124. "Masks"

125. "Metamorphosis"

126. "Miri"

127. "Nemesis"

128. "Night"

129. "Obsession"

130. "One"

131. "Paradise"

132. "Parallax"

133. "Parallels"

134. "Parturition"

135. "Penumbra"

136. "Phantasms"

137. "Progress"

138. "Projections"

139. "Prototype"

140. "Rapture"

141. "Rascals"

SECTION TEN

ANSWERS

STAR TREK: THE ORIGINAL SERIES
ANSWERS

James T. Kirk

1. (a) Gary Mitchell
2. Finnegan
3. *U.S.S. Farragut*
4. (c) "The Enemy Within"
5. Gunpowder and/or a cannon
6. Mugato
7. Kirok
8. (b) Vegan choriomeningitis
9. Romulan
10. Ulysses S. Grant
11. Spock and Leonard McCoy
12. Tarsus IV

Spock

13. True. He served under its previous captain, Christopher Pike, for more than 11 years.
14. First officer and science officer
15. His ears
16. In Christine Chapel's mind
17. T-negative
18. Teacher
19. T'Pring
20. Stonn
21. (d) Sarek
22. (b) "Operation: Annihilate!"
23. (a) A7
24. (d) "Is There in Truth No Beauty?"

Leonard McCoy

25. Bones
26. Plum
27. Chief medical officer
28. (a) "The Corbomite Maneuver"

29. (c) "Journey to Babel"
30. Alice and the White Rabbit from *Alice in Wonderland*
31. The Black Knight
32. (b) Flavius
33. Cordrazine
34. (a) Capella IV
35. (c) Transporter
36. Natira

Montgomery Scott

37. Chief engineer
38. (c) Engines
39. (d) "Who Mourns for Adonais?"
40. (b) Lieutenant Carolyn Palamas
41. Kirk and McCoy
42. *Nomad*
43. Technical journals
44. The *Enterprise*
45. Alcohol
46. (b) Queen to Queen's Level Three
47. (b) "All Our Yesterdays"
48. (d) Scottish

Hikaru Sulu

49. "Where No Man Has Gone Before"
50. (b) Physicist
51. (a) "The Enemy Within"
52. Beauregard
53. A foil (or sword)
54. (d) Landru
55. (c) A samurai
56. "The Return of the Archons"
57. A scar on his face
58. Film (or footage of the *Enterprise*)

ANSWERS

59. (b) "Errand of Mercy"
60. "The City on the Edge of Forever"

Uhura
61. Swahili
62. (c) "The Corbomite Maneuver"
63. Spock
64. *Nomad* erased her knowledge.
65. The alternate Sulu
66. Immortality
67. (c) Shopping
68. Pavel Chekov
69. (c) Lars
70. (a) Elaan
71. Old age
72. Kirk

Pavel Chekov
73. Navigator
74. Russian
75. Leningrad
76. A dead body
77. (d) Yeoman Landon
78. Scott
79. (b) Spock's
80. (d) Tamoon
81. "Spectre of the Gun"
82. Sylvia
83. (c) Piotr
84. Irina Galliulin

Recurring and Guest Characters
85. Spock
86. Dr. Roger Korby
87. Nurse
88. (b) "Turnabout Intruder"
89. "The Naked Time" and "The Conscience of the King"

90. Irish
91. Engineering
92. (a) Tarsus IV
93. (b) Physician
94. (a) Vulcan
95. "A Private Little War" and "That Which Survives"
96. Spock
97. Harcourt Fenton Mudd
98. "Mudd's Women" and "I, Mudd"
99. Leo Walsh
100. (c) Stella
101. (c) Sell tribbles
102. Number One
103. Vina
104. (d) Dr. Piper
105. David Bailey
106. First Federation
107. (a) Iguana
108. "Balance of Terror"
109. (a) Stiles
110. Their androids
111. (b) Andrea
112. Ruk
113. Karidian's daughter, Lenore
114. Kodos the Executioner
115. Jamie
116. Kirk
117. Ensign Garrovick
118. Captain John Christopher
119. Three
120. (d) Lieutenant Marla McGivers
121. (d) One quarter
122. (d) Rigel IV
123. Jack the Ripper
124. Don Juan
125. A Gorn
126. The Metrons
127. (b) Kevas and trillium
128. Commissioner Nancy Hedford

209

129. (d) Apollo
130. Akuta
131. (b) 201 and 347
132. Supervisor 194
133. Alexander
134. Rayna Kapec
135. Mr. Atoz
136. Zor Khan
137. (c) Helen Noel
138. (a) Commodore Stone
139. Droxine
140. (c) Blind

The Original *Enterprise*

141. (a) 203
142. (b) *Constitution*
143. Warp
144. Dilithium
145. Lithium
146. Jefferies tubes
147. Armory
148. Auxiliary control
149. Medical decompression chamber
150. (c) Saucer separation
151. (b) Dr. Laurence Marvick
152. (c) Bowling alley

Crazed Captains

153. Matt Decker
154. Commodore
155. R. M. Merrick
156. (a) Cellular metamorphosis
157. (a) Lord Garth
158. (b) A Vulcan
159. (c) *U.S.S. Exeter*
160. The Prime Directive
161. Immortality
162. Dr. Janice Lester
163. Saurian brandy
164. The Vulcan Death Grip

Supercomputers

165. (a) Kirk
166. (b) Of the Body
167. Eminiar VII and Vendikar
168. Jackson Roykirk
169. (d) *Tan Ru*
170. Vaal
171. The Controller
172. Spock's
173. (d) M-5
174. Dr. Richard Daystrom
175. The Oracle
176. (b) Cygnet XIV

The Captain's Women

177. (c) Helen Noel
178. Miri
179. (a) Janet Wallace
180. Lawyer
181. Marlena Moreau
182. Ruth
183. (c) Clark Gable
184. Andromeda
185. (d) Dohlman
186. (a) Odona
187. (b) Deela
188. Miramanee

Miscellaneous Data

189. Spock
190. Five years
191. (d) Uhura danced.
192. Salt
193. 4,000
194. Dragon
195. (a) iii; (b) i; (c) ii
196. (c) McCoy
197. Shield
198. Fizzbin
199. Troglytes
200. Red

STAR TREK: THE NEXT GENERATION
ANSWERS

Jean-Luc Picard
1. *U.S.S. Stargazer*
2. (c) Heart
3. Q
4. Locutus
5. (b) Commandant of Starfleet Academy
6. A.F.
7. (b) Vineyards
8. The Atlantis Project
9. Dr. Richard Galen
10. A tapestry
11. (a) A saddle
12. (c) Earl Grey tea

William T. Riker
13. Robert DeSoto
14. (b) Betazed
15. (d) Number One
16. Data
17. Minuet
18. (c) Ate Klingon food
19. (a) *U.S.S. Ajax*
20. (c) *U.S.S. Gandhi*
21. (b) Anbo-jytsu
22. (a) Primitive human
23. Lieutenant Commander Shelby
24. (c) Thomas

Data
25. Omicron Theta
26. Noonien and Juliana Soong
27. Lieutenant commander
28. To become human
29. "Datalore"
30. Geordi La Forge
31. (b) Lieutenant Jenna D'Sora
32. "Redemption, Part II"
33. *U.S.S. Sutherland*
34. "Time's Arrow, Part I"
35. (c) Positronic
36. True

Worf
37. Khitomer
38. (b) Mogh
39. Kahlest
40. Lwaxana Troi
41. (a) Gault
42. K'Ehleyr
43. Alexander
44. (b) Guinan
45. A merry man
46. (c) His spine
47. A *bat'leth* competition
48. (a) Sito Jaxa

Deanna Troi
49. Ship's counselor
50. (d) A Starfleet officer
51. Little One
52. Wyatt Miller
53. (c) Ian Andrew
54. (d) Empathic
55. (a) Devinoni Ral
56. (d) "The Masterpiece Society"
57. "Disaster"
58. Romulan
59. *Ode to Psyche*, by John Keats
60. Commander

Geordi La Forge
61. VISOR
62. (a) *U.S.S. Victory*
63. (a) Flight controller
64. (c) Chief engineer
65. "The Arsenal of Freedom"
66. Lieutenant Reginald Barclay

67. (d) *The Pirates of Penzance*
68. Dr. Leah Brahms
69. (b) Alan-a-Dale
70. (a) Haliian
71. Captain
72. Romulan

Beverly Crusher
73. (b) Walker Keel
74. Deneb IV
75. Head of Starfleet Medical
76. How to dance
77. (a) Breakfast
78. (b) Rapidly contracting
79. Howard
80. (a) Candle
81. (b) A healer
82. (c) Arvada III
83. (a) In love with her
84. (c) "Descent, Part II"

Wesley Crusher
85. (a) Stepping on flowers
86. False; he created self-aware nanites
87. (c) Riker and Guinan
88. Picard
89. "Where No One Has Gone Before"
90. "Ménage à Troi"
91. (d) Conn
92. "The First Duty"
93. (c) The Traveler
94. Picard's
95. (b) Nova Squadron
96. Tactical

Natasha Yar
97. Chief of security
98. Data
99. Turkana IV
100. Tasha

101. False; she was orphaned at age five
102. (b) Armus
103. Sela
104. (a) Romulan
105. Worf
106. True
107. (b) "A Matter of Honor"
108. (c) Vagra II

Recurring and Guest Characters
109. Beverly Crusher
110. Riker
111. Three
112. (c) *U.S.S. Repulse*
113. A Sherlock Holmes mystery
114. Transporter
115. (a) Engineer
116. (d) Bendii syndrome
117. *Ancient West*
118. (b) His strength
119. (a) Cytherians
120. (c) Barclay's protomorphosis syndrome
121. "Encounter at Farpoint"
122. Keiko Ishikawa
123. Worf
124. (d) Setlik III
125. (c) *U.S.S. Rutledge*
126. (b) Tactical officer
127. Ten-Forward Lounge
128. (b) Nineteenth
129. The Borg
130. True
131. (a) Terkim
132. (b) Listeners
133. Vash
134. Q
135. (c) Alyssa Ogawa
136. Leonard McCoy
137. Crystalline Entity
138. (d) K'mpec

139. (c) Dexter Remmick
140. Selar
141. Mot
142. Ro Laren
143. (c) Civilian botanist
144. Sela

The *U.S.S. Enterprise* NCC-1701-D

145. *Galaxy*
146. Utopia Planitia
147. (b) Orfil Quinteros
148. 1,000
149. Ready room
150. (b) On the back of the saucer
151. Battle bridge
152. (a) 13
153. Edward Jellico
154. Data
155. "The *Pegasus*"
156. "Cause and Effect"

Q

157. (d) Twenty-first
158. True
159. (c) The power of the Q
160. (b) He wants to join the crew
161. Guinan
162. The Borg
163. (d) Calamarain
164. Lord High Sheriff of Nottingham
165. (b) Crusher
166. (c) Full Q raised as a human
167. (b) Lieutenant
168. Earth

Artificial Intelligence

169. Dr. Noonien Soong
170. (d) His right of self-determination

171. Intelligence, self-awareness, consciousness
172. *Webster's Twenty-Fourth-Century Dictionary*
173. (d) Use contractions
174. Nanites
175. Lal
176. (a) Beloved
177. (d) Six (three prototypes, Lore, Data, Juliana)
178. Professor James Moriarity
179. Exocomps
180. The *Enterprise*-D computer

Miscellaneous Data

181. Away team
182. Riker, La Forge, Crusher, and Wesley
183. (d) Yar and Data
184. Klingons
185. Sarek
186. Pike
187. (b) 2363
188. (a) Klingon
189. (d) The Borg homeworld
190. (b) His combadge
191. (c) "Birthright, Part I"
192. (c) A Jefferies tube intersection
193. Spot
194. Jayden
195. False
196. (b) Rachel Garrett
197. The Mintakans
198. (b) Proto-Vulcan
199. Picard, Data, Troi
200. The Maquis

STAR TREK: DEEP SPACE NINE
ANSWERS

Benjamin Sisko
1. Jennifer
2. Kasidy Yates
3. (b) The Borg
4. Jean-Luc Picard
5. False; Cal was an Academy classmate. Sisko was not known to have had a brother.
6. Emissary of the Prophets
7. (d) Jadzia Dax
8. Curzon Dax
9. (a) *U.S.S. Lexington*
10. A baseball
11. (c) B'hala
12. Lafayette

Kira Nerys
13. (b) Militia
14. Bajoran liaison
15. Shakaar Edon
16. (a) Singha
17. Cardassian
18. Bareil
19. Kirayoshi O'Brien
20. False; Kira always wore a red Bajoran uniform.
21. Colonel
22. "When It Rains . . ."
23. Commander
24. Breen

Odo
25. (c) In the Denorios Belt
26. Dr. Mora Pol
27. Gul Dukat
28. (b) Thrax
29. Constable
30. *Odo'ital*
31. Unknown sample
32. Kira

33. (c) Changeling
34. True; it happened in "Apocalypse Rising."
35. (c) 30
36. Section 31

Quark
37. (d) All of the above
38. *Vulcan Love Slave*
39. (a) Weapons merchant
40. (c) Moon
41. His Marauder Mo action figures
42. He took them out of their original packaging
43. Brunt
44. Morn
45. True; she was Natima Lang.
46. Grilka
47. Rom
48. Ezri Dax

Jadzia Dax
49. Joined
50. (b) Symbiont
51. Boday
52. False; neither was joined.
53. (d) Snacking on tube grubs
54. (a) Arjin
55. (c) Cold hands
56. (c) Icoberry
57. (c) Martok
58. (a) Jake Sisko
59. True; she was first mentioned in "Invasive Procedures."
60. Gul Dukat

Ezri Dax
61. Tigan
62. (d) Spacesick

63. Garak
64. Lieutenant
65. (c) Mining
66. Joran
67. False; she never wanted to be joined.
68. Worf
69. Zee
70. (b) *U.S.S. Destiny*
71. Bashir
72. The Klingon Empire

Miles O'Brien
73. (c) The cello
74. (d) The Battle of Gettysburg
75. "Rumpelstiltskin"
76. (d) The Paradas
77. "Destiny"
78. Darts
79. Chief of operations
80. Nog
81. (a) 20
82. Worf
83. True
84. A teaching position at Starfleet Academy

Julian Bashir
85. Second
86. (c) Jadzia Dax
87. (a) Lost causes
88. Garak
89. (b) A month
90. Kukalaka
91. (b) Genetic resequencing
92. Jack, Patrick, Serena, and Lauren
93. Internal Affairs
94. Felix
95. (d) *U.S.S. Bellerophon*

96. False; Kirayoshi was delivered by a Bajoran midwife.

Worf
97. (a) "The Way of the Warrior"
98. Aboard the *Defiant*
99. The Sword of Kahless
100. Martok
101. Strategic operations officer
102. True; his surname was Rozhenko.
103. Mogh; Martok
104. *Mek'leth*
105. (b) "Change of Heart"
106. (c) The Badlands
107. Gowron
108. Federation ambassador to Qo'noS

Jake Sisko
109. (b) Fishing
110. Nog
111. (c) Go sailing in space
112. (a) 100 gross
113. She was a dabo girl.
114. (d) Melanie
115. *Anslem*
116. The Federation and the Klingon Empire
117. True; it happened in "The Reckoning."
118. (a) Visions
119. (c) Willie Mays
120. *U.S.S. Valiant*

Recurring and Guest Characters
121. Keiko O'Brien
122. A Pah-wraith

123. She was a freighter captain.
124. (a) *Xhosa*
125. True; for smuggling weapons to the Maquis
126. (c) Restaurateur
127. New Orleans
128. (b) Blood screening
129. Elim
130. Obsidian Order
131. (c) Quark
132. Gul Dukat
133. (d) Prefect
134. (b) *U.S.S. Honshu*
135. Technician
136. True; her name was Prinadora.
137. Grand Nagus of the Ferengi Alliance
138. Michael Eddington
139. (a) The Federation
140. Tora Ziyal
141. (a) He drank too much.
142. (b) An amateur sociologist
143. (d) Jupiter Station
144. Kai Winn Adami
145. False; Winn never received visions of the Prophets.
146. General Martok
147. *Rotarran*
148. (a) An eye

Deep Space 9 and the *U.S.S. Defiant*

149. Terok Nor
150. In orbit of Bajor
151. Ops
152. Docking ring
153. 26
154. (a) Runabouts
155. Sisko
156. False; the *Defiant*'s cloaking device is Romulan.

157. (b) The Borg
158. (d) Thomas Riker
159. (b) It was destroyed.
160. Quantum torpedoes

The Dominion

161. (d) "Rules of Acquisition"
162. (c) Morphlings
163. The Vorta
164. The Cardassians and the Breen
165. (b) The blight
166. (b) Omarion
167. The Obsidian Order and the Tal Shiar
168. The Cardassians'
169. 100
170. (b) Quark
171. Betazed
172. True

Bajoran Mysticism and the Prophets

173. (c) Nine
174. Tears
175. (b) Orb shadow
176. (d) Orb of Knowledge
177. (c) Jake
178. Wormhole
179. (a) "The Reckoning"
180. The Pah-wraiths
181. (a) "Destiny"
182. (b) 200
183. *Pagh*
184. True

Miscellaneous Data

185. Tosk
186. (a) A clock
187. (c) The Runners
188. Holograms
189. Odo

190. Jake

191. (d) Odo

192. Garak

193. (c) Bashir

194. Miles O'Brien

195. Bashir

196. Vic Fontaine

197. (d) Breen

198. (c) Bashir

199. *U.S.S. Rio Grande*

Kathryn Janeway

1. (c) Sciences
2. Her father's
3. A lizard
4. (d) *U.S.S. Al-Batani*
5. Q
6. A pocketwatch
7. Tom Paris
8. Ma'am
9. Fresh roses
10. (b) Molly
11. (c) May 20
12. False; Janeway was never married.

Chakotay

13. Captain Sulu
14. A bathtub
15. Medicine wheel
16. Earth's moon
17. (a) His father
18. Seska
19. Commander
20. (b) Venus
21. (d) Temporal mechanics
22. (c) Tom Paris
23. Rubber Tree
24. False; they believed that one "doesn't own anything but the courage and loyalty in his heart."

Tuvok

25. Chief tactical officer
26. T'Pel
27. Four
28. Vulcan Institute of Defensive Arts
29. (c) *U.S.S. Saratoga*
30. *Kal-toh*
31. Lieutenant commander

32. True
33. (b) Blindness
34. That he is a grandfather
35. *Kolinahr*
36. Kes

Tom Paris

37. Eugene
38. Janeway
39. New Zealand, on Earth
40. True
41. (c) Piloting
42. Admiral
43. Kes
44. Land a starship on a planet
45. (b) Twentieth-century pop culture
46. The *Delta Flyer*
47. 1970 Chevy Camaro
48. True; he was lieutenant and then was demoted to ensign.

B'Elanna Torres

49. Chief engineer
50. Kessik IV
51. Dreadnought
52. (b) Vorik
53. (b) Second year
54. She was killed in a Krenim attack.
55. Hoverball
56. Interstellar history
57. "Day of Honor"
58. BLT
59. Klingon
60. True

Harry Kim

61. Libby
62. Operations officer

63. The Delaney sisters
64. (d) Editor of the academy newspaper
65. "Emanations" and "Deadlock"
66. He could literally scare Kim to death.
67. Taresia
68. Paris
69. True
70. (c) Volleyball
71. (c) 8472
72. False

The Doctor

73. Emergency Medical Hologram
74. Dr. Lewis Zimmerman
75. Jupiter Station
76. He is given the power to deactivate himself.
77. Schweitzer
78. Danara Pel
79. His mobile emitter
80. (c) Twenty-ninth
81. (d) Byron
82. Mars
83. (d) Social skills
84. True

Neelix

85. Talaxian
86. (c) Ship's counselor
87. Q
88. The captain's mess
89. *A Briefing With Neelix*
90. False; he claimed to have served his people proudly, but he later admitted that he'd been too afraid to fight.
91. Kes
92. Orbital tethers
93. "Mortal Coil"

94. Nihiliphobia, the fear of nothingness
95. Mr. Vulcan
96. Reginald Barclay

Kes

97. Ocampa
98. (a) Nine years
99. One
100. (b) The Doctor
101. Tuvok
102. Her father
103. (a) Neelix
104. Neelix and Paris
105. (d) Tieran
106. *Elogium*
107. Hydroponics bay
108. (b) 9.5

Seven of Nine

109. Seven of Nine, Tertiary Adjunct of Unimatrix Zero One—but you may call her Seven of Nine
110. Annika Hansen
111. (c) Tendara Colony
112. Regenerates
113. Red
114. (d) Neelix's
115. *Raven*
116. (b) Astrometrics lab
117. (b) "One"
118. Lieutenant Chapman
119. False; she resisted it.
120. (b) Omega molecules

Recurring and Guest Characters

121. Cardassian
122. Kazon
123. Michael Jonas
124. Betazoid

125. Confined to quarters for the rest of the journey home
126. False; he died trying to help the Doctor retake the ship.
127. (a) Sporocystian
128. Suspiria
129. Tanis
130. Sulu
131. Quinn
132. Vulcan
133. Naomi Wildman
134. (a) Xenobiologist
135. (a) Carey
136. Henry Starling
137. (a) Chronowerx
138. Vidiian
139. (b) Annorax
140. A lock of her hair
141. Riley Frazier
142. (d) A Romulan scientist
143. (b) A Cardassian doctor
144. One

The *U.S.S. Voyager*

145. *Intrepid*
146. (d) The Badlands
147. (b) 70,000
148. (a) Bio-neural
149. Landing on a planet
150. (c) Blue
151. (d) Tricobalt explosives
152. "Cathexis" and "Day of Honor"
153. (c) The warp nacelles swing upward.
154. (b) Quantum slipstream
155. True
156. (d) *U.S.S. Equinox*

The Delta Quadrant

157. (d) A quantum singularity
158. (b) A dark-matter nebula
159. It duplicated them
160. True
161. None
162. (b) "Blood Fever"
163. (c) Started a war
164. A Demon-class planet
165. Hirogen
166. The Void
167. (c) Nekrit Expanse
168. (c) Species 8472

Miscellaneous Data

169. (b) Tuvok
170. Quark
171. A wormhole
172. Tuvok
173. Paris, the Doctor, Lon Suder
174. Suder
175. Seska
176. Will Riker
177. Janice Rand
178. Tuvok and Neelix
179. Tuvix
180. Barclay
181. (b) Los Angeles
182. (d) Adrift in space
183. "Scorpion, Part II" and "The Gift"
184. (c) World War II
185. Paris and Seven of Nine
186. Geordi La Forge
187. Pablo Baytart
188. (d) Replicator rations
189. Torres
190. The Borg queen
191. Torres

192. Chakotay

193. The Doctor

194. Seven of Nine

195. *U.S.S. Voyager Shuttlecraft Cochrane*

196. *Challenger*

197. (c) 3,000

198. (c) An automobile

199. A supernova

200. True

STAR TREK: THE FILMS
ANSWERS

The Crew

1. (b) Spock
2. Christine Chapel
3. McCoy
4. Transporter chief
5. McCoy
6. Spock
7. (a) Kirk
8. Captain
9. Three
10. (c) Retnax V
11. Chekov
12. Spock
13. (c) Four
14. (a) Rand
15. (c) *Plak-tow*
16. Sulu
17. David
18. True; to recover Spock's body, Kirk defies orders.
19. Kirk
20. Spock
21. San Francisco
22. Kirk
23. (b) Restore the correct timeline
24. True
25. He missed his old chair.
26. Spock
27. Sarek
28. Chekov
29. Scott
30. False; Kirk refused.
31. Captain of the *U.S.S. Excelsior*
32. (a) A boat
33. (c) David Marcus's
34. (a) 300
35. Murder of the Klingon chancellor
36. Uhura
37. Scott and Chekov
38. Sulu
39. (c) Antonia

40. Guinan
41. (c) Worf
42. (a) His brother and nephew
43. His VISOR was replaced with ocular implants.
44. Picard, Crusher, Worf
45. Data
46. Worf
47. Data
48. True
49. Picard and Worf
50. (a) Several memory engrams
51. Data, Worf, Crusher, and Troi
52. (c) 87.2 centimeters
53. (d) 318 days
54. True

Film Characters

55. Will Decker
56. (c) Sonak
57. Ilia
58. Deltan
59. (b) Missing
60. False; it was *Voyager VI*.
61. Saavik
62. Regula I Space Laboratory
63. He was Kirk's son.
64. Clark Terrell
65. (a) Humor
66. Carol Marcus
67. Starfleet Commander Morrow
68. Sarek
69. Styles
70. (a) Protomatter
71. Saavik and David Marcus
72. (d) T'Lar
73. Federation president
74. Saavik
75. (c) George and Gracie

76. Dr. Gillian Taylor
77. (b) Dr. Nichols
78. Sarek
79. Caithlin Dar
80. St. John Talbot
81. General Korrd
82. (c) To shake his hand
83. Lieutenant Hawk
84. (a) Technology
85. (b) Swimming
86. Artim
87. Ceti eels
88. Kruge
89. (a) Sybok is Spock's brother.
90. Klaa
91. Valeris
92. General Chang
93. Chancellor Gorkon
94. Azetbur
95. Admiral Cartwright
96. El-Aurian
97. Lursa and B'Etor
98. The Borg queen
99. Ru'afo
100. Admiral Matthew Dougherty

Film Ships

101. Weapons console
102. *Surak*
103. Three
104. Third-class neutronic fuel carrier
105. *S.S. Botany Bay*
106. *U.S.S. Reliant*
107. Cloaking device
108. *U.S.S. Excelsior*
109. *U.S.S. Grissom*
110. J. T. Esteban
111. d, c, a, b
112. Klingon bird-of-prey
113. *H.M.S. Bounty*

114. *U.S.S. Saratoga*
115. *U.S.S. Enterprise*
116. *U.S.S. Excelsior*
117. *U.S.S. Enterprise*-A
118. *Galileo* and *Copernicus*
119. *Galileo*
120. False; the *Enterprise*-A was never equipped with transwarp drive.
121. *Kronos One*
122. It could fire weapons while cloaked.
123. *U.S.S. Excelsior*
124. *U.S.S. Excelsior*
125. John Harriman
126. Deck 15
127. Stellar Cartography
128. *U.S.S. Bozeman*
129. 257.4
130. Veridian III
131. Troi
132. *U.S.S. Farragut*
133. *U.S.S. Enterprise*-E
134. *U.S.S. Defiant*
135. *Phoenix*
136. A nuclear missile
137. (d) A scoutship
138. A cloaked holoship
139. Its warp core
140. His captain's yacht

Miscellaneous Data

141. Scott
142. He pawned his antique glasses.
143. On the side of a bus
144. Plexicorp
145. Spock
146. Two
147. (d) Two pairs of gravity boots
148. Yeoman Burke and Samno
149. Valeris

150. (d) A champagne bottle tumbling through space

151. 47

152. Kirk

153. To patrol the Neutral Zone

154. When they realize they're not alone in the universe.

155. Three

156. (d) Lily Sloane

157. Kelbonite

158. They're the same species.

159. (a) Klingons

160. 05

161. (d) In an EVA suit

162. (b) Wrist

163. 2005

164. "Out there. Thataway."

165. A copy of the Charles Dickens book *A Tale of Two Cities*

166. A bottle of Romulan ale, vintage 2283, and a pair of glasses

167. Ceti eel

168. (a) Days = hours

169. One lens had cracked.

170. Reading Klingon

171. True

172. T'plana-Hath, who was quoted in *Star Trek IV: The Voyage Home*

173. "Nothing unreal exists."

174. "How do you feel?"

175. (a) $100

176. Jacqueline Susann and Harold Robbins

177. Too much "LDS" at Berkeley in the '60s

178. (d) Helicopter

179. El Capitan

180. "Because it's there."

181. (d) Weapons

182. Paradise City

183. "To Boldly Go Where No Man Has Gone Before"

184. Spock's birth

185. (a) An icy wasteland

186. (d) Chameloids

187. Crusher

188. Life-forms

189. (a) None

190. Finding Spot

191. (a) Picard's family photo album

192. (b) 9 billion

193. Borg

194. 50 million

195. They hoped to contact the Borg of the twenty-first century.

196. Captain Ahab from *Moby-Dick*

197. 600

198. *H.M.S. Pinafore* by Gilbert and Sullivan

199. She said she'd never kissed him when he'd had a beard.

200. Subspace weapons

NEW LIFE AND NEW CIVILIZATIONS
ANSWERS

Photo Quiz

1. (a) Cardassian (b) Ocampa
   (c) Andorian (d) Vidiian
   (e) Klingon (f) Kazon
   (g) Gorn (h) Trill
   (i) Romulan (j) Ferengi
   (k) Talaxian (l) Tholian

Vulcans

2. "Journey to Babel"
3. (a) 102.437
4. The Vulcan Science Academy
5. Amanda
6. Perrin
7. Skon
8. Solkar
9. (b) Bendii syndrome
10. "Unification, Part I"
11. Six: "Journey to Babel"; *Star Trek III: The Search for Spock*; *Star Trek IV: The Voyage Home*; *Star Trek VI: The Undiscovered Country*; "Sarek"; "Unification, Part I"
12. T'Pau
13. "Dagger of the Mind"
14. The *lirpa* and the *ahnwoon*
15. Every seven years
16. Vorik
17. Green
18. Copper
19. (c) Liver
20. Surak
21. (b) T'plana-Hath
22. A nerve pinch
23. True
24. True
25. Infinite diversity in infinite combinations
26. (c) Mintakans
27. (a) Spock
28. (c) *A Cave Beyond Logic*
29. (c) Has no moon
30. (a) ix; (b) vii; (c) i; (d) vi; (e) viii; (f) iii; (g) iv; (h) ii; (i) v

Romulans

31. Romulus and Remus
32. The Neutral Zone
33. Vulcans
34. (c) 100 years earlier
35. A cloaking device
36. They're Klingon in design.
37. (b) Spock
38. The Right of Statement
39. Romulan ale
40. (b) *Vorta Vor*
41. Treaty of Algeron
42. Cloaking
43. Iconia
44. (b) Over 53 years
45. (a) The Tomed Incident
46. Alidar Jarok
47. (a) The Caves of Mak'ala
48. Tomalak
49. Worf
50. Pardek
51. True; it was Simon Tarses.
52. Artificial quantum singularity
53. They tried to collapse the Bajoran wormhole.
54. Senate
55. Breen
56. Vreenak
57. Gray
58. Neral
59. "Unification, Part II"
60. Telek R'Mor

Klingons

61. (a) Kor
62. (c) Koloth

63. (b) Kang
64. (b) Hikaru Sulu
65. The Albino
66. (Curzon) Dax
67. (c) The Battle of Klach D'Kel Brakt
68. Mara
69. (a) Kor
70. (c) The Sword of Kahless
71. Duras
72. Toral
73. (b) Chancellor
74. The clone of Kahless
75. (a) K'mpec
76. The Cardassian Union
77. Khitomer
78. Worf
79. (c) "In Purgatory's Shadow"
80. Sirella
81. Drex
82. (c) Arne Darvin
83. "The Savage Curtain"
84. (a) Klaa
85. A Klingon moon
86. 50
87. "You Are Cordially Invited . . ."
88. *Anguish*
89. Shakespeare
90. (d) Tear ducts
91. Honor
92. (d) *Ahn-woon*
93. Scream
94. *R'uustai*
95. (c) Is a Klingon opera
96. *Ak'voh*
97. Basai
98. Blood pie
99. (b) *I.K.S. Ya'Vang*
100. (d) Foreplay

Betazoids

101. Daughter of the Fifth House, Holder of the Sacred Chalice of Rixx, Heir to the Holy Rings of Betazed
102. The Sacred Chalice of Rixx
103. "Ménage à Troi"
104. Dr. Timicin
105. Minister Campio
106. Mr. Homn
107. Odo
108. (b) Pregnant
109. *Imzadi*
110. (d) No clothes
111. (c) 10 months
112. Ring a chime
113. Genetic bonding
114. Tam Elbrun
115. (b) Human
116. Plexing
117. The phase
118. Zanthi fever
119. Lon Suder
120. False; Lwaxana married a human and they produced offspring.

The Borg

121. "Q Who?"
122. (d) The Delta Quadrant
123. The collective
124. Drone
125. False; a Borg will only attack someone on its ship who presents a threat
126. Assimilate
127. (b) A cube
128. (b) Cybernetic organisms
129. Third of Five
130. Hugh
131. Lore

132. Sphere

133. (d) 39.1 degrees Celsius

134. Nobility

135. Wolf 359

136. False; no contact between the Borg and the Dominion has ever been established.

137. Chakotay

138. Species 8472

139. (c) Vinculum

140. False; nothing about the Borg in that future was established.

Ferengi

141. True; it happened in "The Nagus."

142. (a) Nog

143. "Bar Association"

144. (c) Miles O'Brien's

145. Jake

146. Jake

147. The Noh-Jay Consortium

148. Losing his leg in battle

149. The grand nagus

150. Ishka

151. (b) Moogie

152. (d) Form a union

153. Liquidator

154. "Family Business"

155. (c) Ishka

156. "The Last Outpost"

157. Rules of Acquisition

158. 285

159. Gold-pressed latinum

160. Dr. Arridor and Kol

161. Ferengi Commerce Authority

162. (c) Gint

163. Pel

164. (b) *Glebbening*

165. (a) *Crisp*

166. An apprenticeship

167. Benjamin Sisko

168. (c) The Abhorred Philanthropist

169. Ferenginar

170. (a) The Sacred Marketplace

Bajorans

171. (b) Advanced tactical training

172. (a) *U.S.S. Wellington*

173. Minister Jaro Essa and Gul Dukat

174. The Prophets

175. Adami

176. Springball

177. (a) A gardener

178. "Life Support"

179. Shakaar Edon

180. Opaka

181. Tahna Los

182. *Kohn-Ma*

183. Li Nalas

184. Navarch

185. (b) The Emissary

186. The Alliance for Global Unity, also known as the Circle

187. Minister Jaro

188. Winn and Bareil

189. (c) The Cardassian takeover of the planet

190. (c) *D'jarra*

191. The Vedek Assembly

192. Bajoran Gratitude Festival or Peldor Festival

193. Bajoran Militia

194. Solar-sail vessels or lightships

195. True

196. True; it happened in "By Inferno's Light."

197. (a) Five months

198. (d) Sneeze a lot
199. (c) 5 million
200. (b) *Bantacas*

Cardassians
201. Elim Garak
202. Detapa Council
203. Tora Ziyal
204. Tora Naprem
205. (b) *Groumall*
206. True; Kira's mother sacrificed herself during the occupation in exchange for food and medicine for her family.
207. Bajoran
208. He was struck blind.
209. He became a tailor.
210. True; it happened in "The Die Is Cast."
211. Dr. Julian Bashir
212. Romulus
213. Tora Ziyal
214. (c) Head
215. Enabran Tain
216. "Empok Nor"
217. False; it was never established that Garak was ever married.
218. Dukat
219. Ziyal
220. "Tacking into the Wind"
221. False; Damar was killed in the final hours of the war.
222. Arawath Colony
223. "In Purgatory's Shadow"
224. Dominion internment camp 371
225. (d) Gul Darhe'el
226. Aamin Marritza
227. Rugal
228. Natima Lang
229. The True Way
230. *Meditations on a Crimson Shadow*

231. (b) The repetitive epic
232. *The Never Ending Sacrifice*
233. (a) Kotra
234. (b) "Death to all."
235. (a) Arid

Trills
236. "The Host"
237. Ambassador Odan
238. Symbiosis Evaluation Board
239. Initiates
240. (d) Field docent
241. Jadzia Dax
242. (b) The guardians
243. Reassociation
244. False; such friendships rarely survive a change of host.
245. *Zhian'tara*
246. Rite of emergence
247. (c) 1 in 1,000
248. (d) One in two
249. Isoboramine
250. (c) The wormhole
251. Nilani
252. Verad
253. Kell Perim
254. (c) Electrical discharges
255. (a) Heat

Vorta
256. (b) Weyoun Four
257. (b) Shot by a Ferengi
258. (d) Weyoun Seven
259. The Founders
260. (a) Telekinesis
261. (d) To save the life of a Founder
262. (c) Deyos
263. (a) Keevan
264. (b) Luaran
265. (d) Yelgrun

Jem'Hadar

266. (c) Ketracel-white
267. Odo
268. Goran'Agar
269. Obedience
270. (b) Life
271. (b) A first
272. (b) 30 years
273. (d) An honored elder
274. (c) Shroud
275. One faction was created in the Gamma Quadrant; the other was created in the Alpha Quadrant.

Founders

276. (c) Tzenkethi
277. (b) Krajensky
278. (b) A Romulan
279. Gowron
280. (d) The lure of the Great Link
281. Section 31
282. Odo
283. Laas
284. Kira
285. True

Delta Quadrant Life-Forms

286. Talaxian–Haakonian war
287. False; it's one of Neelix's favorite rituals.
288. (c) Laxeth
289. (a) Paxim
290. (a) Wixiban
291. (b) Paxau resort
292. The Caretaker
293. (b) The array
294. The Kazon

295. Tanis
296. (a) Pranik
297. A food replicator
298. (a) Seska
299. (c) Maje
300. The Trabe
301. True; it happened in "Basics, Part I."
302. The phage
303. His lungs
304. The Vidiian Sodality
305. (b) *Honatta*
306. Split her in two, one human and one Klingon
307. (c) The think tank
308. The Borg
309. Kes
310. Borg nanoprobes
311. Fluidic space
312. None; they don't sleep.
313. (c) Five
314. (c) Communications relay stations
315. Tuvok and Seven of Nine
316. Quantum singularity
317. A member of species 8472
318. To practice hunting for the *Voyager* crew
319. World War II occupied France
320. The Malon
321. Theta
322. The Vori
323. The Kradin
324. (a) The Tak Tak

Hybrids

325. (a) vi; (b) iv; (c) vii; (d) ix; (e) ii; (f) viii; (g) i; (h) iii; (i) v

STARFLEET
ANSWERS

Starfleet Academy

1. San Francisco
2. John Gill
3. Korrd
4. Valeris
5. Mordock, T'Shanik, Oliana Mirren
6. Mordock
7. Walter Horne
8. Boothby
9. Saturn
10. Nova
11. Joshua Albert
12. Kolvoord Starburst
13. Cortin Zweller and Marta Batanides
14. Warp
15. Calvin Hudson
16. Solok
17. Miles O'Brien
18. James Mooney MacAllister
19. Daniel Byrd
20. Professor Chapman
21. Space walks
22. Class-2 claustrophobia
23. 54 years
24. Quantum Cafe
25. True; the first time, he was made an ensign; the second time, he was made a lieutenant.

Starfleet (General)

26. Spock
27. (b) 7
28. San Francisco
29. The right of an individual who is accused of a crime to remain silent.
30. (c) Communications with an approaching vessel
31. (b) 15
32. (d) 46A
33. Worf
34. Data
35. Commander Bruce Maddox
36. Admiral's Banquet
37. Nog
38. Blood screenings
39. Starfleet Intelligence
40. The Doctor

The Federation (General)

41. The Prime Directive
42. T'Pau
43. Memory Alpha
44. Federation Archaeology Council
45. The Maquis
46. (b) 150
47. The New Essentialists Movement
48. (b) Bajorans
49. The Federation Council
50. Paris

Diplomacy

51. Coridan's admission to the Federation
52. The Orions
53. Parliament
54. Riva
55. (a) Antedeans
56. (c) Between 300 and 400
57. Tin Man or Gomtuu
58. Will Riker
59. "Darmok"
60. Legarans
61. Ambassador Spock
62. The Cardassians

Command

63. (a) iii; (b) v; (c) ii; (d) i; (e) iv

64. Dr. Janice Lester
65. Commodore Robert Wesley
66. Paul Rice
67. Walker Keel
68. Tryla Scott
69. Lieutenant Richard Castillo
70. (b) Picard
71. Admiral Alynna Nechayev
72. Erik Pressman
73. "The Adversary"
74. Lisa Cusak
75. Rudy Ransom

Medicine

76. A martini
77. "The living and the dying"
78. Dr. Tristan Adams
79. Dr. Simon Van Gelder
80. Dr. Leonard McCoy
81. Selar
82. Beverly Crusher
83. PCS, or Pulaski's Chicken Soup
84. Dr. Julian Bashir
85. False; Bashir obtained the cure from Luther Sloan.
86. *Voyager*'s EMH
87. Danara Pel
88. Joe Tormolen
89. Physical contact
90. Adrenaline
91. Hyronalin
92. Pavel Chekov
93. (a) Heart
94. Tri-ox
95. A neural paralyzer
96. Lexorin
97. It allowed her body to grow a new kidney.
98. Immediate postprandial upper abdominal distension

99. Cramps
100. Chemotherapy and funduscopic examinations
101. Iverson's disease
102. Radiation exposure
103. Felicium
104. Cryogenics
105. His Aunt Adele
106. Cardiac replacement
107. Radiation poisoning
108. An analgesic cream
109. He mistook a preganglionic fiber for a postganglionic nerve.
110. Kalla-Nohra syndrome
111. An alien cheese
112. Metremia
113. Holotransference dementia syndrome—when you spend so much time in a holoprogram you think it's real
114. It could leave its host's body and grow to several feet in size.
115. Medical triage

Sciences

116. (a) An oxygen–nitrogen atmosphere
117. Salt
118. Borgia plant
119. Venus drug
120. Pergium
121. (d) A sickly-sweet odor
122. Hemoglobin
123. Ultraviolet radiation
124. Spores
125. Kironide
126. Dilithium crystals
127. Styrolite
128. A cosmic string fragment
129. Trilithium resin
130. (a) A nuclear inhibitor

131. The unusual metaphasic radiation coming from the planet's rings
132. Protouniverse
133. Wormhole
134. Verterons
135. Harvesters
136. A spatial scission
137. The theory of infinite velocity
138. Symbiogenesis
139. Class Y
140. Theta radiation

Technology

141. Transtator
142. Tricorder
143. The corbomite device
144. Baffle plate
145. Neural neutralizer
146. Transmuter
147. His mirror
148. Cross-circuited to "B"
149. The Teacher
150. (d) Terraforming
151. Transwarp
152. Six inches
153. The keyboard
154. Macintosh Plus
155. (c) A pager
156. He planted a viridian patch on Kirk.
157. A magnetic shield
158. Using a resonance burst from the main deflector dish
159. Antigrav
160. Universal translator
161. Antigrav
162. Isolinear optical chip
163. Annular confinement beam
164. Ferroplasmic infusion
165. The Custodian

166. A snake's-head walking stick
167. Dyson Sphere
168. Transporter
169. Anyon emitter
170. Psi-wave device
171. Metaphasic-shield technology
172. A neuroprocessor
173. An interplexing beacon/subspace transmitter
174. The moon's gravitational field
175. A phase variance in his positronic matrix
176. A duonetic field
177. Metreon cascade
178. The Talaxians
179. The Talaxian moon Rinax
180. The isograted circuit
181. Interferometric dispersion

Travels in Space and Time

182. A transporter
183. Black star
184. "Assignment: Earth"
185. *Star Trek IV: The Voyage Home*
186. The Guardian of Forever
187. An atavachron
188. A wormhole
189. (b) 8,000
190. Berlinghoff Rasmussen
191. (c) Twenty-sixth
192. The Iconians'
193. Warp 5
194. Gabriel Bell
195. Temporal causality loop; predestination paradox
196. 17
197. Folded-space transport
198. Temporal

199. The Borg
200. (b) Soliton wave

Astrometrics
201. 11
202. Talos IV
203. Alfa 177
204. Exo III
205. Thasus
206. Tarsus IV
207. Argelius II
208. Babel
209. Capella IV
210. Archanis IV
211. Eminiar VII
212. Ardana
213. Ceti Alpha VI
214. Mutara Nebula
215. Genesis Planet
216. Mount Seleya on Vulcan
217. Nimbus III
218. In the Neutral Zone
219. Yosemite National Park
220. Camp Khitomer, near the Romulan border
221. Deneb IV
222. Angel One
223. Aldea
224. Klingon outpost Narendra III
225. Risa
226. Galorndon Core
227. The nexus
228. Amargosa
229. Veridian III
230. Veridian IV
231. Tycho City, New Berlin, Lake Armstrong
232. The Briar Patch
233. Denorios Belt
234. The Badlands
235. Jeraddo

236. Dominion internment camp 371
237. Gaia
238. Adigeon Prime
239. Ajilon Prime
240. Alastria
241. Azure
242. Drayan II
243. (d) Delta

Starships
244. *S.S. Columbia*
245. *Fesarius*
246. *U.S.S. Antares*
247. *Astral Queen*
248. *U.S.S. Republic*
249. *U.S.S. Intrepid*
250. *U.S.S. Archon*
251. Experimental prototype
252. *U.S.S. Stargazer*
253. *U.S.S. Tripoli*
254. *U.S.S. Yamato*
255. *U.S.S. Enterprise*-C
256. *Constellation* class
257. *U.S.S. Rutledge*
258. *U.S.S. Hera*
259. *U.S.S. Pegasus*
260. *U.S.S. Defiant*
261. *Phoenix*
262. *U.S.S. Defiant*
263. *Quark's Treasure*
264. *Aeon*
265. (b) *U.S.S. Prometheus*
266. (a) Split into three independent ships
267. *Relativity*
268. *U.S.S. Equinox*
269. *Nova*-class science vessel
270. (a) x; (b) v; (c) iv; (d) ix; (e) viii; (f) iii; (g) i; (h) vi; (i) vii; (j) ii
271. (a) iv; (b) v; (c) ii; (d) i; (e) iii

Chronology

272. 1930
273. 1990s
274. (c) 18 months
275. 1996
276. 15 years
277. (b) Six months later
278. Eighteenth-century American
279. Three years, classifying gaseous planetary anomalies in the Beta Quadrant
280. 27 years
281. Stardate 9529.1
282. 78
283. 34
284. Nearly a year
285. Mid-twenty-first century
286. April 4, 2063
287. April 5, 2063
288. 0.8 seconds
289. 309 years
290. 1950s
291. 1937

Court of Law

292. Samuel T. Cogley
293. (b) Books
294. Murder
295. Article 184
296. Colonel Worf
297. Life sentence in the dilithium mines of the penal colony of Rura Penthe
298. Starfleet Judge Advocate General Phillipa Louvois
299. Dr. Nel Apgar
300. Apgar himself, while trying to kill Riker
301. Admiral Norah Satie
302. Ibudan
303. Enina Tandro
304. Kira Nerys

305. True
306. O'Brien
307. Archon
308. Nestor
309. A life sentence at the Lazon II labor camp
310. He was made a solid.
311. Argrathi
312. Firing on a civilian Klingon vessel and killing all aboard
313. Ch'Pok
314. Sisko
315. He had to relive the murder again and again.
316. A terrorist bombing
317. "Aggravated violent thought . . . resulting in grave bodily harm"

Secret Groups

318. Admiral Gregory Quinn
319. V'Shar
320. Federation Department of Temporal Investigations
321. Dulmer and Lucsly
322. The Orion Syndicate
323. Liam Bilby
324. Tal Shiar
325. Koval
326. Admiral Ross
327. Enabran Tain
328. Kira Nerys
329. Orias system
330. The Tal Shiar
331. Section 31
332. Luther Sloan

Alternate Timelines and Parallel Universes

333. (c) A beard
334. Agonizer
335. Tantalus field
336. Captain Pike

337. (d) It was made of anti-matter.

338. Natasha Yar

339. Worf and Deanna Troi

340. Ensign

341. Klingons

342. Data

343. Deanna Troi

344. K'mtar

345. Cardassians and Klingons

346. Intendant

347. Smiley

348. Regent of the Klingon Empire

349. Korena

350. (c) Nog

351. Morn

352. Yedrin

353. (a) iii; (b) vii; (c) viii; (d) xi; (e) iv; (f) xii; (g) i; (h) vi; (i) xiii; (j) ix; (k) x; (l) v; (m) ii

354. (c) *Galaxy*

355. (c) Kes

356. Harry Kim and Tom Paris

357. (b) A security officer

PERSONNEL FILES
ANSWERS

Relativity

1. David Marcus
2. George Samuel Kirk
3. Peter Kirk
4. Sarek
5. Amanda
6. Sybok
7. Skon
8. Solkar
9. David McCoy
10. Demora Sulu
11. Maurice Picard
12. Yvette Gessard Picard
13. Robert Picard
14. René Picard
15. Adele
16. Kyle Riker
17. Ishara Yar
18. Sela
19. Felisa Howard
20. Ian Andrew Troi
21. Lwaxana Troi
22. Kestra Troi
23. Sergey Rozhenko
24. Helena Rozhenko
25. Nikolai Rozhenko
26. Mogh
27. Kurn
28. Alexander Rozhenko
29. Jack Crusher
30. Joseph Sisko
31. Sarah Sisko
32. Judith Sisko
33. Jennifer Sisko
34. Kira Meru
35. Kira Taban
36. Kira Reon, Kira Pohl
37. Richard Bashir
38. Amsha Bashir
39. Molly
40. Kirayoshi
41. Keldar

42. Ishka
43. Rom
44. Nog
45. Yanas Tigan
46. Norvo Tigan, Janel Tigan
47. Kolopak
48. Alixia
49. Martis
50. Benaren
51. Magnus
52. Erin
53. Lela
54. Tobin
55. Emony
56. Audrid
57. Torias
58. Joran
59. Curzon
60. Jadzia
61. Ezri

Pets and Other Animals

62. Tango
63. (d) *Sehlat*
64. Cat
65. Isis
66. (d) Whales
67. Blue whales
68. (c) Blue unicorns
69. Cat
70. *Targ*
71. Lwaxana Troi
72. *Lapling*
73. Corvan gilvos
74. A cat
75. Lieutenant Reginald Barclay
76. An iguana
77. Lycosa tarantula
78. A lionfish
79. Butler
80. *Star Trek Generations*

81. *Palukoo*
82. Martok
83. Mark

Crew Hobbies
84. Three-dimensional chess
85. (c) Gun collecting
86. (d) Ezri
87. (c) Participating in gymnastics
88. Picard
89. Fermat's last theorem
90. Stratagema
91. Riker
92. Building ships in bottles
93. *Henry V*
94. (d) Riker
95. Wesley and Robin Lefler
96. Baseball
97. Jadzia
98. *Tongo*
99. (c) Giving
100. A Bajoran solar-sail ship
101. Sisko
102. (a) Worf
103. *Finding and Winning Your Perfect Mate*
104. Dabo
105. Dom-jot
106. O'Brien and Bashir
107. Fizzbin
108. O'Brien
109. Go Fish
110. Pool
111. (c) Sculpting
112. The Doctor

Food and Drink
113. *Tranya*
114. A bowl of *plomeek* soup
115. His chicken sandwich and coffee

116. Pizza and beer
117. "Marsh melons"
118. Romulan ale
119. Dom Pérignon 2265
120. Earl Grey, hot
121. Apple
122. Arcturian Fizz
123. Anything chocolate!
124. Prune juice
125. 10
126. Ensign Sonya Gomez
127. Fungilli
128. Picard
129. Green
130. Deanna Troi
131. (b) *Hasperat*
132. He hated it.
133. *Raktajino*
134. Bajoran springwine
135. Bloodwine
136. (d) Chew it
137. Azna
138. *Jumja*
139. (b) A Cardassian drink
140. *Yamok* sauce
141. Tube grubs
142. *Angla'bosque*
143. Coffee

Holoprograms
144. "The Big Goodbye"
145. Madeline
146. His cousin Gloria from Cleveland
147. Professor James Moriarty
148. Geordi La Forge
149. Dr. Katherine Pulaski
150. "Elementary, Dear Data" and "Ship in a Bottle"
151. "Goddess of Empathy"
152. Parallax Colony on Shiralea VI

153. Worf and Alexander
154. Deadwood, South Dakota
155. Durango
156. Sir Isaac Newton, Albert Einstein, and Dr. Stephen Hawking
157. Reginald Barclay
158. Beverly Crusher
159. On the nineteenth-century frigate *Enterprise*
160. 12
161. 13
162. Fishing in the holosuite
163. Altonian brain teaser
164. Dr. Hippocrates Noah
165. Kira Nerys
166. Vic Fontaine's casino
167. Vegas, 1962
168. Felix
169. Vic Fontaine
170. Chez Sandrine
171. Tom Paris's
172. *Beowulf*
173. Kathryn Janeway
174. B'Elanna Torres
175. Tuvok
176. Seska
177. Leonardo da Vinci
178. Captain Proton
179. Chaotica
180. Janeway

Music of the Spheres

181. (a) iii; (b) v; (c) iv; (d) vi; (e) vii; (f) i; (g) ii
182. "I'll Take You Home Again, Kathleen"
183. "Beyond Antares"
184. Harpsichord
185. Yeoman Teresa Ross
186. Spock
187. Adam
188. "Amazing Grace"

189. "I Hate You"
190. "Row, Row, Row Your Boat"
191. "Pop Goes the Weasel"
192. "If I Only Had a Brain"
193. Dixieland, because you can't dance to it
194. Being made immortal again
195. "Night Bird"
196. "Frère Jacques"
197. "The Inner Light"
198. "The Minstrel Boy"
199. Data
200. (d) He cried.
201. Hector Berlioz
202. "Ooby Dooby," by Roy Orbison
203. "Moonlight Becomes You"
204. "Magic Carpet Ride," by Steppenwolf
205. "A British Tar"
206. A mambo
207. "Louie, Louie"
208. "They Can't Take That Away from Me"
209. "The Best Is Yet to Come"
210. *"O soave fanciulla"*
211. "Falor's Journey"
212. "Echoes of the Void"
213. "You Are My Sunshine"

Youth

214. A bottle of her favorite perfume
215. Three photos of Rand
216. Three-dimensional chess
217. Onlies
218. Grups
219. The Horta
220. The Gorgan/Friendly Angel
221. His nephew, Peter
222. Seven

223. Hunger strike

224. Hedril

225. Nog

226. Worf

227. The *morrok*

228. Neelix

229. Seska

ABSTRACT KNOWLEDGE
ANSWERS

Voiceprint Identification

1. (d) Landru
2. "Let me help."
3. Lincoln
4. A tribble
5. "That is best served cold"
6. Spock
7. Montgomery Scott
8. Worf
9. The Enterprise-A
10. The Borg
11. "Darmok and Jalad at Tanagra"
12. Family
13. "Some days the bear gets you"
14. Female Shape-shifter
15. (c) Joseph Sisko
16. (b) Ishka
17. Garak
18. Benny Russell
19. "Please state the nature of the medical emergency."
20. Chakotay
21. (d) lots of money
22. Q
23. "Impossible"

Identify the Episode

24. "Tomorrow Is Yesterday"
25. "Accession"
26. "The Adversary"
27. "All Good Things . . ."
28. "One"
29. "Allegiance"
30. "Statistical Probabilities"
31. "Alter Ego"
32. "Basics, Part I"
33. "The Alternative Factor"
34. "Amok Time"
35. "And the Children Shall Lead"
36. "Angel One"
37. "The Deadly Years"
38. "The Apple"
39. "Arena"
40. "Armageddon Game"
41. "The Arsenal of Freedom"
42. "The Ascent"
43. "The Assignment"
44. "Before and After"
45. "Attached"
46. "Babel"
47. "Ex Post Facto"
48. "Darkling"
49. "Alliances"
50. "Is There in Truth No Beauty?"
51. "Turnabout Intruder"
52. "Looking for *par'Mach* in All the Wrong Places"
53. "The Measure of a Man"
54. "All Our Yesterdays"
55. "Assignment: Earth"
56. "The Q and the Gray"
57. "Time's Arrow, Part I and II"
58. "The Naked Time"
59. "Apocalypse Rising"
60. "The Abandoned"
61. "A Private Little War"
62. "Hero Worship"
63. "Aquiel"
64. "The Next Phase"
65. "Battle Lines"
66. "The Forsaken"
67. "The Alternate"

Episode Titles

68. (c)
69. (c)
70. (b)
71. (d)
72. (a)

240

73. (b)	**115.** (d)
74. (c)	**116.** (d)
75. (d)	**117.** (b)
76. (b)	**118.** (b)
77. (d)	**119.** (b)
78. (a)	**120.** (b)
79. (c)	**121.** (d)
80. (c)	**122.** (d)
81. (b)	**123.** (d)
82. (d)	**124.** (b)
83. (b)	**125.** (a)
84. (b)	**126.** (a)
85. (b)	**127.** (d)
86. (d)	**128.** (d)
87. (c)	**129.** (a)
88. (c)	**130.** (d)
89. (c)	**131.** (c)
90. (d)	**132.** (d)
91. (c)	**133.** (b)
92. (b)	**134.** (d)
93. (d)	**135.** (c)
94. (d)	**136.** (b)
95. (c)	**137.** (c)
96. (d)	**138.** (d)
97. (b)	**139.** (d)
98. (c)	**140.** (c)
99. (b)	**141.** (b)
100. (b)	**142.** (c)
101. (c)	**143.** (b)
102. (d)	**144.** (d)
103. (c)	**145.** (d)
104. (c)	**146.** (d)
105. (b)	**147.** (c)
106. (d)	**148.** (d)
107. (c)	**149.** (b)
108. (b)	**150.** (d)
109. (c)	**151.** (d)
110. (b)	**152.** (c)
111. (d)	**153.** (c)
112. (d)	**154.** (b)
113. (c)	**155.** (c)
114. (b)	**156.** (b)

157. (b)

158. (b)

159. (d)

160. (d)

161. (b)

162. (b)

163. (c)

164. (d)

165. (d)

166. (d)

167. (b)

168. (c)

169. (c)

170. (c)

171. (c)

ACKNOWLEDGMENTS

I'd like to give a special thank-you to Ken Barr of Ambrosia Books and Collectibles in Los Angeles, the Time Meddlers of Los Angeles, Gallifrey Conventions in Los Angeles, and Galileo Conventions in London for being so supportive of me and of my first book, *Quotable Star Trek*.

Thanks to Joe Menosky, Bryan Fuller, Rob Doherty, and Mike O'Halloran for helping me with tapes and scripts and for answering my questions.

And always, my appreciation to the wonderful people at Pocket Books, especially my editor, Marco Palmieri, Margaret Clark, and Scott Shannon.

A final acknowledgment must go to Mike and Denise Okuda (and their *Star Trek Encyclopedia*) for being the true archivists of all things Star Trek.

ABOUT THE AUTHOR

Jill Sherwin is the author of *Quotable Star Trek,* a contributor to *The Lives of Dax,* and a former assistant to the writers/ producers of *Star Trek: Deep Space Nine.* She is currently working as a freelance writer. Along with her books, she counts her proudest achievements as being her mom's kid and her dog's dad.